Dream Destinations

Falling in love all over the world!

This year, you are invited to experience the wonders of Iceland and Costa Rica in Sophie Pembroke's latest jet-set duet!

Prepare to be dazzled by the blue lagoon, hot springs and dramatic landscape of Iceland as Hollywood stars Winter and Josh are reunited once again at the opening of a luxury hotel. Can the memories of their broken fairy-tale marriage be healed this time around?

And then lose yourself in the sultry rain forest and hide away among the towering trees in a tree house where hotelier Liam and personal assistant Jenny come face-to-face with the repercussions of their one unforgettable night together in Costa Rica!

Both available now!

Dear Reader,

We all need a break from time to time—a chance to step back from real life and relax. And while we can't always jet off to a Costa Rican rain forest to hang out in a luxury tree house, take long walks along a beach or spot sloths on a trail to a heart-stopping waterfall, we *can* all find ten minutes to imagine ourselves there!

Reading is the best way I know to travel to other places and live other lives—and to fall in love over and over again. So while I can't hand you a plane ticket right now, I hope you'll curl up with Jenny and Liam's story and escape to that tree house, and enjoy their Costa Rican adventures!

Love and waterfalls,

Sophie x

Baby Surprise in Costa Rica

Sophie Pembroke

HARLEQUIN

Romance

Recycling programs for this product may not exist in your area.

ISBN-13: 978-1-335-73708-3

Baby Surprise in Costa Rica

Copyright © 2023 by Sophie Pembroke

For questions and comments about the quality of this book, please contact us at CustomerService@Harlequin.com.

Harlequin Enterprises ULC
22 Adelaide St. West, 41st Floor
Toronto, Ontario M5H 4E3, Canada
www.Harlequin.com

Printed in U.S.A.

Sophie Pembroke has been dreaming, reading and writing romance ever since she read her first Harlequin as part of her English literature degree at Lancaster University, so getting to write romantic fiction for a living really is a dream come true! Born in Abu Dhabi, Sophie grew up in Wales and now lives in a little Hertfordshire market town with her scientist husband, her incredibly imaginative and creative daughter, and her adventurous, adorable little boy. In Sophie's world, happy *is* forever after, everything stops for tea and there's always time for one more page...

Visit the Author Profile page
at Harlequin.com for more titles.

To everyone who needs a holiday right now...

**Praise for
Sophie Pembroke**

"An emotionally satisfying contemporary romance
full of hope and heart, *Second Chance for the
Single Mom* is the latest spellbinding tale from
Sophie Pembroke's very gifted pen. A poignant
and feel-good tale that touches the heart and lifts
the spirits."

—*Goodreads*

CHAPTER ONE

JENNY BOUCHARD STEPPED out of the four-by-four that had delivered her from the airport and felt the heat—and the fear—hit her as the air-conditioned bubble of denial the car had provided so far fell away.

I'm really doing this.

I must be losing my mind.

Around her, the Costa Rican jungle seemed alive with sounds—the breeze through the trees making the leaves whisper, the chirping of insects and the calls of unfamiliar birds echoing. If she closed her eyes, she might still be on the plane, or even back in her LA apartment, listening to her rainforest playlist as she tried to sleep.

But she didn't close her eyes. Instead, she scanned her surroundings for the place she'd travelled thousands of miles to visit—and the man she'd come here to find.

'This does *not* look right,' she murmured to herself as she turned slowly, searching for signs of the luxury treehouse resort she'd expected to be there.

Nothing.

Why was she even surprised? It wasn't as if she didn't already know that men were all promises and no delivery. Except he hadn't promised *her* a luxury treehouse resort—he'd promised his investors. And in her experience men tended to be far more loyal to money than to women.

Jenny pulled her light, sleeveless blouse away from her already sticky skin and considered her options. Just like she'd been doing for the last month or more—ever since the third pregnancy test returned the same answer as the first two: *pregnant.*

First off, she needed more information. She turned back to the airport transfer car to ask the driver if he was *sure* this was the right place, but the four-by-four was already pulling away, back onto the dusty road out of there, towards the city. Eyes widening, she chased it for a few steps, but the driver never looked back, or even checked his mirrors.

At least he'd left her suitcase behind, leaning neatly against the nearest tree. She peered at the trunk, then strained her neck to stare up at the leaf canopy, trying to figure out what sort of tree it was. She'd done some research on this area of Costa Rica, this particular stretch of tropical rainforest that ran along the Caribbean coast, learning about the biodiversity of the area, the transport options, the cuisine—she didn't like to travel unprepared.

Except, it seemed, for the fact that the luxurious treehouse resort she'd come to visit didn't exist.

The website had been stunning—full of promises of a remote retreat getaway location, with yoga and mindfulness sessions, trips to nearby waterfalls or zip lines through the rainforest, local restaurants down by the beachfront, snorkelling, rainforest safaris…

And luxury treehouse accommodation. That had been a definite—a place to stay. She wouldn't have come otherwise.

Of course she hadn't been able to actually book a room on the website. But she hadn't thought she'd need to.

Josh and Winter had said that Liam was down in Costa Rica, at his latest resort property, and shown her the website. And she knew, from the time she'd spent in Iceland with Liam at his *last* new resort, that he always reserved a suite of rooms for his personal use. So she'd figured she'd stay with him—especially since, generous as she was, Winter didn't pay her enough in her role as PA to afford Liam's resort prices anyway.

But now there was no sign of Liam. And no sign of the treehouses.

This is what people do. They let you down.

How had she forgotten that, even for a moment?

Perhaps she could blame pregnancy brain.

She pulled her cell phone from her pocket and was just trying to decide who she could call when she heard a laugh from further down the track that led deeper into the rainforest. A familiar laugh, rising above the bird cries and the insects and the buzz of humidity that filled her ears. A laugh she'd last heard low in her ear as Liam teased her to the brink in his private hot spring lagoon…

Maybe she wasn't in the wrong place after all.

Grabbing her suitcase, Jenny set off further down the track, looking for any sign of the structures and promises the website had given her. She didn't spot anything to reassure her—no *Welcome to Paradise* signs or a nice, friendly reception hut or anything. But she heard more voices—shouts and calls and laughs—so she pushed on anyway.

One last turn and she entered a clearing in the trees, abuzz with activity. Building materials—mostly wood of varying sorts, from what she could tell, and ropes—were neatly piled around the space, and a group of men had gathered at the far side of the clearing, all too focused on something going on in a large, sturdy tree to notice her.

'Okay, let's do this!' She recognised Liam's voice as his words rang out, but she still couldn't see him. 'On three!'

The countdown echoed through the trees and suddenly a smaller group pulled on a rope Jenny hadn't spotted, and something flew up from the ground towards the tree canopy. She jumped back, even though she was already a safe distance away, a smile stretching her lips as she realised what it was.

A bridge, made of rope and slats of wood, leading from one treetop to another. She squinted up into the canopy again and saw the base of a treehouse in the first tree, obviously still a work in progress.

The website hadn't lied, then. It had just been a little...premature.

This place was going to be amazing, she realised with delight. Totally different to the Ice House Hotel in Iceland, but spectacular in its own way. She could see why Liam was apparently so excited about it.

'Secure!' Liam yelled. He must be up in the tree, Jenny realised. 'Coming down!'

And suddenly all the fear that had been mounting in her gut since she'd landed in Costa Rica came back with a vengeance.

Not finding Liam here in the rainforest would have been bad, sure. But right now she wasn't convinced that finding him was going to be any better.

Gripping the handle of her suitcase tightly with sweaty palms, she forced herself to focus. She was here to do a job and get out. A courtesy visit, that was all this was. She knew Liam—well, no, that was a lie. But she knew enough to know that he wasn't looking for a family, or anything resembling a relationship right now. Of course, she hadn't been either. That much they'd made clear to each other before they began their…rendezvous in Iceland.

She was under no impression that her news was going to be welcomed. But that didn't mean she wasn't under a moral obligation to share it.

She needed to tell Liam about the baby, so that she could plan her future and move on. Until she'd told him, everything was in flux. Uncertain. And Jenny hated not knowing, not being in control of what happened next, more than anything.

She'd given up her power over her own future once before, trusted a man she thought loved her to take care of things, and it had almost ruined her life. She had absolutely no intention of doing it ever again.

Jenny thought of the small silk pouch at the bottom of the rucksack she'd used for hand luggage, and her grandmother's battered and worn Tarot cards inside it. Grandma had believed they could tell the path of a person's life if read correctly—something Jenny had never really bought into. They'd never been able to tell *her* future, or she'd have been better prepared for this eventuality, and the long series of personal disasters and failings that had led her here.

But she *did* believe Grandma when she'd told her the cards could explain her *present*. Because the pictures they held were all stories, and they could be read any way the dealer wanted. When she looked at the cards, she picked out the issues and the images that were already on her mind, and they helped her find clarity of thought.

That wasn't why she kept the cards, of course. She kept them because they were the only thing she had left of her Grandma, of a family that had loved her, once upon a time.

But it was why she'd pulled them out on the plane and shuffled them, feeling their worn edges soft under her fingers, and turned over the first three cards onto the fold-down table of the seat in front.

Past, present and future, Grandma would have said, but Jenny knew they were all here, right now. Hindsight, experience and fear might be better words. Hope, if she was feeling really optimistic.

Which she wasn't, currently.

The cards hadn't told her anything she didn't already know.

First, she'd pulled Judgement for the past. She'd drawn that one for Winter before they went to Iceland too, she remembered—told her it was the card of consequences and reckoning, but also of rebirth and metamorphosis. That it asked a person if they were ready to face their past and move on to their future.

She let her hand rest against her stomach. It wasn't as if she had much say in whether she was ready or not, was it?

The last card, the future card, had been the Wheel of Fortune. A reminder of the unpredictability of life, and that everything changes. Again, not a new concept.

And between them both, in her present position, had been the Knight of Wands. The card her Grandma had whispered was the *naughtiest* card in the Tarot. Jenny hadn't understood why when she was younger. It was only when she matured that she realised how damn sexy it really was. The Knight of Wands was the card of undeniable chemistry, inexplicable attraction—of the pull of that one person you knew you should stay away from but just couldn't resist…

Basically, everything Liam had been for her

since she'd met him in Iceland nearly three months ago.

And any moment now she'd be seeing him again.

As she watched, a figure swung his way down from the tree where the rope bridge had been secured, barely even using the ladder leaning against it to descend. She recognised his body before his face; with his shirt off, the planes of his back and then his chest as he turned were so familiar from those days in Iceland...if rather more tanned than she remembered. Sweat ran in rivulets through the dust that covered his body, and Jenny felt her mouth turn dry and knew it had nothing to do with the Costa Rican heat.

She swallowed and raised her gaze, taking in his dark hair, dulled by sawdust, and his bright blue eyes—and the moment he spotted her standing across the clearing.

Here we go...

Liam Delaney stared across the clearing in the Costa Rican rainforest and tried to figure out if he was hallucinating. He'd been working hard, these past few weeks, and now it seemed like his dreaming self had taken over his waking one.

That, or Jenny Bouchard—the one-week fling he hadn't quite managed to get out of his head, or his dreams—had sought him out for a replay of their time together in Iceland.

He took in her blonde hair, caught up in a high ponytail that left her neck bare as it cascaded down her back, the sunglasses perched on her nose in place of her usual black-framed specs, and the sleeveless blouse and khaki shorts she wore with her trainers.

She looked real. And in his dreams she was usually wearing a lot less. Smiling more, too.

It was really her.

Liam brushed aside the questions from the crew about what was next. The day was getting away from them anyway, and they all deserved an early finish. The cheer that went up when he told them they were done for the day confirmed his hunch that they wouldn't mind.

He left them clearing up, ready for tomorrow, and crossed to where Jenny stood, watching him.

'You know, when Josh told me you were here getting your next resort hotel ready to open, I was kind of expecting the place to at least be built already,' she said, folding her arms over her chest as he got closer.

'I like to be hands-on from the very start.' He stopped in front of her, letting his gaze roam over the curve of her neck, the swell of her breasts under that thin blouse. All the places he'd only had his memory to remind him of until now.

'I remember.' Her voice lowered with the words, and Liam knew he wasn't imagining the flash of heat in her eyes.

It had been the same the day they'd met in Iceland. She'd somehow manoeuvred him into carrying her bags and showing her the suite she was sharing with Winter, and he'd known immediately that he was going to be doing whatever this woman wanted for the whole week she was staying at his hotel. The connection, the chemistry between them, had been instantaneous, and undeniable.

And when he'd met her gaze as he was leaving the room shortly after, he'd known from the unsettled expression on her face that she'd felt it too—and was as surprised by it as he was.

Now she'd surprised him again, showing up here unannounced. God, he hoped this wasn't some sort of 'can't live without you' desperation thing. They'd both been very clear about what their week in Iceland meant—a good time and nothing more.

He wasn't in the market for anything more.

His concern must have shown on his face, because Jenny gave him a sly smile and said, 'How worried are you right now that I'm here to pronounce undying love and propose to you?'

'Little bit,' he admitted, and she laughed.

It was that sound that put his mind at rest most of all. Jenny had the filthiest laugh of any woman he'd ever met, and he loved it. Loved the promise in it—as well as the memories it brought back.

She wouldn't laugh like that if she was there for anything more than a booty call. Would she?

'So, what brings you to my neck of the rainforest?' he asked, as casually as he could. 'I mean, if it's not your sudden inability to live without me?'

'I had a week off.' She shrugged, and Liam found himself suddenly distracted by the movement of that thin blouse over her breasts. 'And Josh mentioned your next project was

somewhere hot for a change, so I thought…
well. I'm betting you can imagine what I
thought.'

He studied her face and saw that same
warmth in her smile, that promise behind
it, but there was something in her eyes that
was less familiar. She was holding something
back.

Was she really here to see him, or to avoid
something else?

Not my problem.

He wasn't her boyfriend, or her brother—
thank God. He was just a guy she'd known
for a week and had a lot of fantastic sex with.
Well, he'd thought it was fantastic, and if her
showing up here was a sign of anything,
surely it was that he was right about that?

Whatever her problems were, he couldn't
fix them. But he *could* give her a fun week
off—and himself a well-deserved break at the
same time. The crew could manage without
him for a few days, he was sure.

And maybe a few more days with Jenny
would be enough to get her out of his system at last, and stop him dreaming about her
every bloody night. They just hadn't let their
fling run its full course, that was all, before

she'd had to leave to go back to LA with Winter and Josh. And even when they'd been together they'd been distracted, dealing with her boss and his best friend rekindling their long dead marriage—and helping out a little, behind the scenes.

But Winter and Josh weren't there now. It was just the two of them, in the middle of a rainforest. What kind of an idiot would he have to be to not take advantage of the situation she'd given him?

'Well, as you've noticed, the resort isn't actually completed yet—or open to the public,' he said. 'But lucky for you, there is *one* finished treehouse here for you to stay in, if you'd like.'

He leaned in closer and whispered the word in her ear. '*Mine*.'

CHAPTER TWO

LIAM'S PERSONAL TREEHOUSE was set a bit further back into the rainforest. Jenny assumed this was so that, even when the whole resort complex was complete, he'd still have some privacy—something she'd noticed in Iceland mattered a great deal to him.

Perhaps she should have considered that before descending on him in the middle of nowhere with no warning. But if she'd told him she was coming...he might have told her not to. And the news she had to share with him, well, it didn't feel like something she could do over the phone.

Or at all, right now. Her courage had faded the moment she saw that cautious smile on his lips and she'd realised he was worried she was there for *commitment.*

Which she wasn't. At least, not for herself. As she trailed after him along the track towards his treehouse, Jenny tore her attention away from the muscles in his bare back, and his ass in those low-riding shorts, and forced herself to focus on what she was there to do.

Tell Liam that he was going to be a father and ask if he wanted to be involved at all in the child's life.

She was prepared for him to say no. Hell, she was expecting it. Liam had never given her any indication that he wanted anything more from her than a few nights of great sex—and that was all she had wanted too.

But it seemed the universe had other ideas. And now they had to deal with them.

The only question was how. She knew she had to give Liam a chance to be involved but, honestly, she was banking on his saying no. If he said no, she could set out to figure out her own future alone, and have it under her control.

Far better for him to say no now, and never meet their child, than to decide to bail later, once the kid was already attached.

Jenny knew how that felt. Her own family had abandoned her just when she needed them the most, because she didn't live up to their ideals of what a daughter should be. There was no way in hell she was putting her own child through that.

If Liam said yes, he wanted to be part of the kid's life, then changed his mind later...

'Here we are.' Liam paused at the foot of a broad, hefty-based tree. It took Jenny a moment to spot the staircase running around the outside of it, and for a second it looked like he'd placed his foot on a tree root and just intended to climb. 'It's perfectly safe, I assure you.'

'It's beautiful.' Jenny stepped back to take in the full effect, now she knew that it was there.

The spiralling stairs were made of wood, like everything else she'd seen so far, but the narrow banister that was in place to protect people walking up them was made from twisted tree roots and rope, intertwined with live foliage to give more cover. It was only when she tilted her head right back and looked up that she could see the base of a treehouse—a larger one than the structures being built in the clearing—stretching back between this tree and several others behind it.

If she hadn't been looking, she might have continued through the rainforest without ever realising this house was there, it was so well camouflaged by its surroundings.

Liam flashed her a smile—that one that made her legs feel just a little weak. 'Come on up.'

She gripped the tree root railing and followed him up the stairs that spiralled around the tree trunk, perfectly angled to avoid anyone hitting their head as they approached the platform that housed Liam's rainforest home.

Jenny had to admit to a certain amount of curiosity as to what sort of place he'd built here. The hotel in Iceland had been cutting-edge in style with see-through glass elevators and stairs, stark modern Scandi styling in the bedrooms and every luxury made available. From what she knew of his other retreat resorts—in the US and overseas—they also focused on luxury for their elite customers. But she couldn't quite see how that kind of luxury would translate to the middle of a Costa Rican rainforest.

Stepping into the treehouse from the wooden porch at the top of the platform, it was instantly clear that Liam had managed it, though.

Where the Iceland hotel had taken its inspiration from the unique landscape, the grey skies and the snow, and the local culture, so too did the treehouse. But, instead of stark neutrals and glass, here the style and texture was far more natural.

The main room of the house, suspended between three huge trees, was an open-plan living-dining-kitchen space, with wooden walls, floor and roof. It should have been confining, or too much, but the mix of colours and grains to the wood somehow lifted it beyond that feeling she'd expected of standing inside a children's playhouse. Of course, the furnishings helped too.

Everything remained neutral, just as in Iceland, except here those neutrals were warm creams and browns and ochres, and used in squishy-looking sofas and textured rugs. The open shelving in the kitchen was stacked with what looked like local pottery and glassware, and any functional items—like a dishwasher and fridge—were hidden away behind pale wooden doors.

Then there was the view. Each of the walls was left open to a balcony that ran almost the full circumference of the living space, save where the stairs were. There were windows that could be closed, but Jenny wasn't sure why you ever would, when you could be so connected to the world outside.

Without a word, she slipped through the open doors onto the balcony and leaned against the twisted wooden railing, feeling the knots and grain of the wood under her skin. From up here in the tree canopy it felt as if she was part of the world of the birds and animals who inhabited the rainforest. The sound of their calls, their rustling in the leaves, surrounded her and she found herself more at peace than she'd been in weeks.

Since Iceland, really. Since she'd lain in bed with Liam Delaney, completely sated, after he'd comprehensively taken her mind off any worries she might ever have had.

She'd never had sex that stopped her brain functioning until she met Liam. That stopped her planning and thinking about the future.

'You like it then?' he asked from behind her now, and it took her a moment to remember that he was talking about the accommodation, not sex.

She turned to face him with a smile. 'It's gorgeous.'

Then she swallowed as she realised she could as easily be talking about him as the treehouse.

He was still topless, which didn't help, his skin part dull with dust and part sheened with sweat. The tan he'd acquired since relocating from Iceland to South America gave a new definition to his lightly muscled torso, and Jenny found it hard not to remember every moment she'd spent touching his skin with her hands, her mouth, every inch of her body.

And here inside there was no audience to make her feel bad about ogling. Liam certainly didn't seem to mind the attention, if the smile that spread across his face was any indication.

She twisted back around to stare out over the rainforest canopy rather than acknowledge his knowing smile. 'It feels like I'm really part of the rainforest up here.'

'That's what I was aiming for.' He moved to stand beside her, and she couldn't help but look at his muscled forearms against the wood, rather than the wonders of the natural world around her. 'And if you like feeling part of the scenery here, I should tell you that the rainforest shower in the bathroom is spectacular.'

He didn't look at her as he spoke, but Jenny grinned at the not-so-subtle undertones of his words all the same.

'Is that so? I look forward to trying it out, especially after a long day's travelling. But really, I think you need the shower more than me right now.'

Liam looked down at his dust and sweat-smeared torso. 'You may have a point. But then, we are all about conservation and eco-tourism around here. We should probably try to find a way to save water...'

She needed to tell him about the pregnancy tests. About the baby. About being a father.

But the moment she did...things would change, just like they had for her the moment she held that positive test in her hands. And she wasn't ready for that, not yet.

Was it so greedy of her to want just one more night—or afternoon, really—with Liam Delaney?

Perhaps. But she was taking it anyway.

Shifting to face him as she leaned against the railing, Jenny met his gaze head-on. 'Seems to me there's only one answer,' she said. 'We'll just have to share.'

Next time Liam built himself a new suite of rooms at his latest resort, a shower big enough for two was definitely going to be a priority.

Not that the rainforest shower he'd installed

in the treehouse wet room was anything to sniff at. With the wide, square shower head above, and some miracle of water pressure, the warm water falling on them really did feel almost like rain. And honestly, with Jenny's bare body pressed up against him—wet and warm and willing—he wasn't really thinking all that much about the shower anyway.

Just that he wished he had slightly more room to do everything he wanted to do to her right now...

Jenny trailed a soapy washcloth over his shoulders, following it with her mouth as the soapsuds washed away, and he bit back a moan at the sensitive tingles in his skin as she reached the dip above his collarbone. God, he'd thought he'd remembered exactly how good she was at this, but it seemed even his dreams couldn't live up to the real thing.

Any concerns he'd had about why she'd hunted him down to Costa Rica had disappeared the moment she took up his hinted invitation to share a shower. *This* was why she'd come. Because they were bloody incredible together, and just the feel of her body against his was enough to put him right on the brink.

It had been weeks. Months, even. And as

much as he appreciated the slow, teasing approach, she was going to have to save it for round two.

Liam grabbed her around the waist, spinning her against the tiles of the wet room and pressing her to them with his kiss against her mouth, before moving his way down her neck. 'This shower really isn't big enough for what I want to do to you.'

'I think we're probably clean enough by now, don't you?' she gasped back.

'One last check...' Dropping down to his knees, he kissed his way across her breasts, her stomach and down to her thighs, before surging up between her legs with his tongue.

'Oh!' He felt her thighs tense and relax under his hands. 'I suppose I can live with that.'

With a grin, Liam went to work, savouring every second as the rainforest shower from above ran rivulets down his back and face. Oh, he remembered this. How responsive she was. How perfectly she reacted to everything he tried. It didn't take long to bring her to the brink...and stop.

She slapped a hand lightly against his shoulder. 'That's it?'

'That's starters.' He slammed his hand against the button to switch off the water, then reached for a fluffy towel from the hook on the far side of the room. He didn't bother wrapping one around himself—the air was hot enough that he knew he'd dry in seconds. But he took a few moments to run the towel over Jenny's body, knowing how hypersensitive she'd be right now, how every touch would just remind her of what she was aching for.

Him. Inside her.

It was very important that she not forget that before they reached the bed.

'Enough,' she said, her voice raspy, and he dropped the towel to the floor. 'Bed. Now.'

'As you wish.'

Later, he'd take time to show off the views from the wide, wide window that spanned the whole width of the bedroom. To let her admire the size of the bed he'd had to build up here, build the room around almost, because there was no way to carry one so big up the stairs—the mattress had been a battle enough. Later, there'd be time for all sorts of things.

Right now, all Liam could think about was burying himself in her again.

She tugged him towards the bed and he took just a moment to admire her body, the familiar curves and dips, the softness of her pale skin. That gorgeous blonde hair hanging darkly wet over her shoulders, almost covering the breasts he'd forgotten were quite so full.

He knelt on the edge of the bed, half over her, as he reached across to the bedside drawer and pulled out a condom. Beneath him, Jenny tensed for a second, then relaxed, and he decided not to question it. If she was worried about who he'd been with since her, she needn't be. There hadn't been anyone, although he didn't like to think too much about why.

His dreams had been too full of her to want anyone else. Clearly that was something else to try and get out of his system this week.

Protection in place, he rested on his elbows above her, smiling down. 'I missed you, you know.'

Her return grin was impish. 'I missed this.' And then she was reaching out and guiding him inside her, and Liam knew that none of the rest of it mattered right now.

Live in the moment, that was his philosophy these days. And God, what a moment to live in.

From the moment he felt her around him, Liam knew there was no way this was going to take long. Neither of them had the patience to take it slow any longer, not this time. Still, he drew it out as best he could, until he felt her start to tighten around him with her orgasm, and his hips started to stutter and he couldn't hold off his pleasure a moment longer.

Collapsing half on top and half beside her with a grin, he waited for his heart to return to a normal tempo, and considered that, really, he might as well have waited to take the shower until afterwards, since he was clearly going to need another one now.

'I don't know what made you decide to come all the way down here,' he said, skimming a hand across her side and over her breasts. 'But I'm damn pleased you did.'

He brought his hand down a little to rest against her belly, and felt her tense under his hand. Frowning, he looked up to see tension in her face too—jaw tight, eyes wary.

He was missing something here. And he hated that.

'Jenny…'

She shook her head. 'Don't—' She broke off.

Oh, whatever this was, Liam was damn sure it wasn't going to be good. He pushed himself up to sit beside her, removing the condom before staring her straight in the eye.

He almost didn't want to ask. But not knowing would be worse, somehow.

'Why did you come to Costa Rica? The real reason, this time.'

She winced and looked away. Looked down. At her stomach.

His whole brain was screaming *no*. But she obviously couldn't hear it, because she kept talking.

'Because I'm pregnant.' She looked up and met his gaze again. 'And you're the father.'

CHAPTER THREE

SHE WAS WATCHING Liam unspool before her very eyes. Not that she blamed him; that wasn't *exactly* the way she'd prepared herself to share the news on the plane. And she definitely hadn't planned to be naked when she did it, but pregnancy hormones were a real thing. So was the stupid chemistry between them that had got them into this mess in the first place.

And now, here they were. Both naked. Him horrified, eyes wide and mouth open. Her guilty and regretful and, although she'd deny it if asked, a little disappointed.

She shouldn't be. She'd known, coming here, exactly how this was going to go. She'd practised the conversation in her head plenty of times, and felt pretty confident filling in Liam's lines for him.

I'm pregnant, she'd say. *And you're the father.*

You're sure? he'd reply, and it wouldn't really be a question, because Liam wasn't that sort of guy. He wasn't marriage and babies and happy-ever-after material, but that was okay because neither was she. But he wasn't someone who'd skip out on his responsibilities or try to deny them. And he wouldn't pressure her either. *What do you want to do?* he'd ask.

I want to keep it, she'd tell him, firmly. *And I'm happy to do that alone. I know this isn't what we agreed, or what either of us planned for. I'm not here to demand anything or blame anyone. I'm here as a courtesy, to let you know, so you can be involved if you want. Otherwise, I'll walk away and raise my child and never bother you again.*

She'd practised that part over and over in the mirror until she could say it without her voice wobbling. Going it alone was scary, no denying that. But she'd done it before—started her life over without anyone by her side. She could do it again, and this time with a baby too.

Doing it alone was better than trusting people who could let you down. *Would* let you down, in the end. She'd trusted a man she'd loved before. She'd trusted that her family would always love her no matter once.

She had no intention of making that mistake a third time.

So Liam would nod, consider. Maybe he'd ask for a little time to think, and she'd give him that graciously. But, eventually, she knew what would happen next.

I'm not cut out to be a father, he'd say eventually. *I can't be part of this.*

And then she'd know.

Sometimes when she pictured it he'd offer her money—a lump sum, or a regular allowance. Sometimes he'd even go as far as asking for updates, or to be told when the kid started asking questions about their father. Others, he washed his hands of the whole thing and signed away all parental rights. It depended on how optimistic she was feeling on the day.

The point was, however she pictured it, their conversation was always cordial. Businesslike, even.

And she was always, always wearing clothes.

Liam blinked, for the first time in an age, then rolled off the bed and stalked into the bathroom without a word—presumably to get rid of the condom and clean up. Maybe even get dressed.

Jenny would love to do the same, but since her clothes were *in* the bathroom, and her suitcase abandoned somewhere in the living space by all the very open windows, she didn't have that option. Unless…

With a quick glance towards the bathroom to check he wasn't coming back already, Jenny dived into the drawers beside the bed—noting in passing how they looked like they were carved directly into the tree trunk that she now realised served as part of one of the bedroom walls—and pulled out a clean white T-shirt and a pair of grey boxers. Dressing quickly in them, she felt more prepared to face whatever Liam had to say next.

When he emerged, he had a towel wrapped around his waist and his hair was damp again. He glanced briefly at the bed, and she saw a twitch at his jaw as he realised she'd stolen his clothes, but he didn't say anything. Instead, he crossed to the drawers himself and pulled out another set of the same and dressed in them, before turning again to face her.

The silence between them made her uncomfortable. From the moment they'd met in Iceland there hadn't been silence between them—just teasing and banter and light, inconsequential conversation.

But the conversation they needed to have now was anything but inconsequential.

She tried, desperately, to remember her well-rehearsed speech—but every word went out of her head when she saw the confusion and disappointment in his bright blue eyes.

'I meant to tell you before, well… I meant to tell you *first*,' she said. 'I guess I just got a little carried away in the moment.'

His harsh laughter told her what he thought of *that* understatement.

'We were careful,' he said, finally. 'In Iceland. We took precautions.'

Jenny nodded. 'We did.' It had been her first thought too. That this *couldn't* happen, because they'd been so damn careful to make sure it didn't. 'But no contraceptive is foolproof. You know that.'

'I do.' A sharp nod. 'Okay. I'm not going to bother asking if you're sure it's mine. I won't insult you like that. You wouldn't be here if it wasn't.'

She acknowledged that with a dip of her head. At least *one* part of this was going to plan. She hadn't completely misjudged him after all.

'And you're keeping it, I assume,' he went on. 'Or, again, why come all the way to the middle of nowhere to find me?'

'Yes.'

'So. What is it you want from me, exactly?' There was an edge in Liam's voice she didn't like, a coldness that transcended the heat of the rainforest. How ironic that their time together in Iceland had been filled with heat and passion, warmth and friendship. And now they were here in Costa Rica in the sweltering heat, Jenny felt like she needed a sweater to protect her from the ice in his eyes.

She took a breath and forced herself to focus on the words she'd practised. She'd had her one last tumble with Liam, and she was under no illusion that he'd ever want her that way again, not now. All she needed to do now was rip the sticking plaster off, get the answer she knew was coming, and then she could be on the next plane out of South America and get home to LA and her job and her life.

She'd have to figure out how to tell her boss that she'd accidentally got pregnant by

Winter's husband's best friend, but that was a bridge for later.

First she had to cross this one.

'You're right; I'm keeping the baby. And I'm happy to do that alone. This wasn't what we agreed in Iceland, and it definitely wasn't what either of us planned for. But I'm not here to demand anything from you. I'm here as a courtesy, to let you know, so you can be involved if you want. Otherwise, I'll walk away and raise my child and never bother you again.'

There. She'd said it.

Now she just needed to remember to keep breathing while she waited for his answer.

Liam stared at her, his insides swirling and his mind a fog, as he tried to make sense of her words. Of everything that had happened since he'd spotted her across the clearing earlier that day.

I'll walk away and raise my child and never bother you again.

He should take that option, he knew it. Hand over a chunk of cash and opt out of the whole fatherhood thing. It was the easiest option. The sensible option. The safe option.

The one that wouldn't break his heart, or the hard-fought-for peace of mind he'd finally achieved.

This isn't what either of us planned.

Understatement. This was the exact opposite of everything he'd planned for his life, ever since that day five years ago where his whole world collapsed and he wasn't sure he'd ever crawl out of the hole it left behind.

The world knew about the accident; it had been in enough papers and magazines, photos splashed all across the internet. They knew Liam had been lucky to escape that car crash with his life. And they knew that his girlfriend, who'd been driving, hadn't been so lucky.

The world didn't know that she'd been pregnant at the time. That Liam hadn't just lost his love but his future in that moment.

They didn't know that it was his fault either.

Jenny couldn't know all that; even Josh didn't know the whole of it, and Liam trusted him enough not to have shared what he did know with anyone.

She'd know that he'd walked away from Hollywood after that, probably even have heard that he went off the rails for a while—like he hadn't been halfway there already. And she knew what he did next, of course—setting up retreat hotels for burnt-out and wayward creatives to find themselves again, along with a lot of high-paying tourists.

But she wouldn't, couldn't, know how the news of her pregnancy would blindside him. And if he got his way, she never would.

He marshalled his thoughts, trying to stop them spinning around in some variation of *why?* and *how?* and *what now?*

When he spoke, he managed to keep his voice even and calm, which he was pretty damn impressed with, personally. 'Let's not either of us do or say anything rash.'

Perching himself against the windowsill, he watched her curled up against the headboard, dressed in his boxers and T-shirt, and felt his unruly body reacting to the sight again. As if that wasn't what had got them into this mess to start with.

'If you only came here as a courtesy, to tell me the situation, what was…this?' He gestured between the two of them. If she'd hoped to use sex to manipulate him one way or the other, he would be very disappointed in how badly he'd misjudged her.

She pulled a face. 'I told you. I got—*we* got carried away. It wasn't like I intended to show up here and jump back into bed with you. It was just...old habits, I suppose.'

Old habits, with someone he'd only met for the first time less than three months ago. It should be laughable. But he took her point.

It wasn't like there'd been anything much to their relationship *outside* the bedroom, when they'd met.

There never was, for him.

He had rules now, since the accident. Liam Delaney's rules for living, ones he'd never share with another person, but that he followed rigidly. Because when he didn't, that was when his life fell apart again.

Some rules could be bent, maybe a little. Others could be updated as circumstances changed. As long as he knew the rules he was operating by, and reminded himself of them often, he could stay on the right path. Grounded, safe, and no danger to himself or anybody else.

The number one rule, though, that could never be changed. *That* was the rule that underpinned his entire existence in this *after-wards*. Life after the accident. If he let *that* rule slide…he didn't want to imagine what would happen then.

Rule number one: never care too deeply about anything or anyone that can be taken away from you.

It was the loss that had nearly killed him. The yawning emptiness that had filled his insides and drained away everything that made life worth living.

He wouldn't survive losing another thing he loved. So he wouldn't let himself love anything.

It was as simple as that.

And for five years that rule had been easy to follow. He was discreet in his relationships, and always upfront about what he was offering. It had taken a while for him to even think about getting back in the game, so it wasn't as if there had been that many women since, anyway.

Jenny had been an unexpected delight; his plans for that week in Iceland had all been about promoting his new hotel, and helping two of his best friends find closure on their failed marriage. And if he'd been hoping they might both see what idiots they'd been to walk away from the love they'd shared, well, he'd got lucky there.

He wasn't against love for everyone. Just him. He didn't have the strength to withstand it.

Meeting Jenny had been more than luck; it had felt like fate. With the Iceland hotel up and running, and the Costa Rica project stalled at the time, he'd been desperate for a distraction. And Jenny, with her blonde ponytail, knowing smile and a line in flirtatious banter that drove him wild, had been just what he needed.

The fact that her wants and desires for any liaison between them—fun, sex, friendship, and then say goodbye at the end of the week—had dovetailed exactly with his had only cemented his belief that their fling was meant to be.

And it had been perfect, right up to the friendly goodbye they'd said the moment she'd left. They'd both known that there was a good chance they'd see each other again— she worked for his best friends, after all— and maybe they'd pick up where they'd left off when they did. But there was no expectation, no obligation.

No risk.

Because while he liked Jenny, he didn't love her—he hadn't even opened himself up to the possibility of that, and besides, who really fell in love in a week? Not Liam Delaney, he knew that much.

He'd been safe.

Until now.

Because as much as he trusted himself not to fall in love with Jenny, or any other woman, a baby was a different matter.

He hadn't changed so much from the man he'd once been that he believed he was capable of not loving his own child.

And that was the biggest risk of all.

So what the hell was he supposed to do now?

CHAPTER FOUR

CLEARLY THIS HAD been a mistake. Coming to Costa Rica. Sleeping with Liam again. Hell, even letting him seduce her in Iceland. Or, well, seducing him, actually.

All of it. Every last minute had been a mistake.

But especially thinking, even for a moment, that he'd appreciate her coming all this way to tell him he was about to be a father.

Coming here for sex? Sure, he'd thank her for that. But doing the morally right thing and telling him about the baby?

From the look on his face, he wasn't in the slightest bit grateful for that.

She pushed off the bed and made a move towards the bathroom to look for her clothes. 'I should go. If I head straight back to the airport I think there's another flight back to LA tonight.' She had no idea if that was true or not, but right now she'd rather sleep in one of those plastic airport chairs and wait until morning than stay another moment in this ridiculously luxurious treehouse with *him.*

She'd expected him to let her down. She hadn't expected it to hurt.

'Wait.' He moved faster than she'd anticipated, blocking her path to the bathroom so fast she almost crashed into him. 'I'm not saying... I just... I need time to think.'

'Time to figure out how to say you don't want anything to do with this, you mean?' Because of course he didn't. And she was furious with herself for letting herself think, however briefly, that he might.

'No. Look.' He raked a hand through his dark hair, leaving it looking even messier than usual. 'You've had...how long to think about this?'

'A month,' she admitted. 'Maybe six weeks.'

'And you needed that time to get your head around things before you came to see me, right?'

She nodded. 'I guess.'

Reaching out, he encircled her wrists lightly with his fingers and looked directly into her eyes. 'I'm not asking for a month, Jenny. I just… I can't think straight right now. And I need to think straight if we're going to figure out what happens next.'

'That's fair, I suppose.' She shook her hands loose and stepped away, towards the warm breeze from the window. It was harder to think when he was touching her. Her body got in the way of her brain.

He wasn't throwing her out. Wasn't demanding he never see her or the baby ever again. He just needed a little time. She'd expected that, hadn't she?

And she could give him that, to a point. After all, babies came with their own timetable. If she was going to head back to LA and figure out her future, she needed to know where she stood with him. What his expectations were, if he had any.

She couldn't live with not knowing where she stood for very long.

'I can give you a week,' she said, finally. 'After that, I need to be back at work in LA. And I need the time before the baby comes to figure out what I do next.'

'A week.' Liam nodded. 'I can work with that.' He sounded confident, but then he always did. Looking closer, she could see the doubt in his eyes.

There was no room for uncertainty in this debate though, so Jenny spelled it out a little clearer. 'By that, I mean we have one week to figure out our future, and the future of our child.'

His eyebrows shot up. '*Our* future.'

Of course his brain went there. Jenny rolled her eyes. 'I'm not trying to trap you into marriage or anything here, Liam. I just mean that by the end of this week I need to know what the future looks like. If this kid is going to have two parents or one, for instance.'

'Right.' He looked uncomfortable at the reminder that he could still walk away, while she really couldn't. Or wouldn't.

'At the end of this week either we'll have a plan I can work with for co-parenting, one that lets me plan my future with some certainty, or I'll walk out of your life for ever, and you'll sign all parental rights over to me. Okay?'

She could tell from the muscle pulsing in his jaw that it *wasn't* okay, but he was going to have to get okay with it real quick. Because this was what she needed and, since she was the one carrying the kid, he was going to have to work with her on this.

'Is that all of your demands?' he asked tightly.

Jenny was about to nod when she thought of something else. Something that had already derailed her plans once and couldn't be allowed to again.

But she had a feeling he *really* wasn't going to like this condition.

'Not quite,' she said. 'While we figure this out…there can't be anything else between us.'

'Anything else? Like what?'

So much for hinting. 'Sex. We can't have sex again until we come to an agreement on the baby.'

He blinked once, really slowly, as if the concept made no sense to him at all. Maybe it didn't. She'd fallen into bed with him the moment she'd seen him again, after all. It was kind of a change of pace.

'No sex.' His mouth twisted, as if he'd just sucked on a lemon. 'Can I ask why?'

'It's too distracting,' she said shortly. She wasn't about to tell him everything that had happened the last time she'd let her libido override her brain. When she'd let her inexperience convince her that sex meant love, and that two bodies bumping together could only lead to fairy tale endings.

Instead, it had cost Jenny her job, her family, her reputation, her self-esteem—her future. Fighting her way back from that was her biggest achievement to date.

She wouldn't let the chemistry between her and Liam put her back where she'd started again.

Now, his lips curved up into a smile. 'Is that so?'

The man really didn't need his ego stroking any more, but Jenny had a feeling he'd be testing this boundary all week if she wasn't very, very clear about her reasoning. Or as clear as she could be without confessing all her past mistakes.

'When we're touching each other, or kissing, or more…it's too much. I can't think straight.'

'Which explains why you failed to mention that you were pregnant until *after* we had sex today.'

'Just like I told you,' she snapped back. He was sounding far too pleased with himself for her liking.

'So you did.' His smile only grew. 'I had no idea that my sexuality was so…potent.'

'*Our* chemistry has been a distraction right from the start. For both of us.'

He acknowledged the point. 'True. It is…' He trailed off, apparently unable to find a word to accurately describe that strange connection that had snapped between them from the moment they'd met.

'It's distracting,' she finished for him, repeating her earlier word choice rather than picking any of the others that sprung to mind. *Overwhelming. Incredible. Mind-blowing.*

'And neither of us can afford to be distracted when making a decision as important as this,' Liam said, surprising her. 'I can't say I'm not disappointed, but I take your point.'

'Good.'

He pushed away from the bathroom doorway, where he'd been leaning, and shifted to one side to allow her access to her clothes. She didn't move towards them though. Not yet.

'So, we're agreed,' she pressed. 'One week to make this decision. And no sex.'

'Until the decision is made,' Liam said. 'Yes, we're agreed.'

She nodded sharply, trying to look as businesslike as was possible when she was wearing the man's boxer shorts. 'Okay, then. I'll just…' She darted past him, into the bathroom, shutting the door quickly behind her.

Gathering her clothes up from the floor, she caught sight of herself in the mirror. Her hair had dried into messy waves, as if she'd spent the day at the beach, and her skin was pink and flushed—from the sex or the argument, she wasn't sure.

Either way, she looked like she'd just been…well, doing exactly what she *had* been doing, and the sight of it, and the memories it awoke, made her blood warm all over again.

One week. I've just got to keep my hands— and lips—off him for one week. For the sake of my future. And our baby.

She gave herself a stiff nod in the mirror and set the shower to cool before she stepped in to clean up again.

One week. She could do that.

Couldn't she?

Liam retreated to the living area when he heard the shower start. Obviously Jenny was taking a little time, and putting some space between them, before they had to figure out what happened next. He couldn't deny he was grateful for it.

At first, he'd been taken aback by her requirement for no sex until they'd resolved the issues between them. He'd even wondered if it was a threat or an attempt to seduce him into making the right decision—withholding sex unless he did.

Except Jenny hadn't given him a *right* decision that she wanted him to make. As long as he decided one way or the other, it seemed like she'd be happy. Should he be insulted that she didn't care if he wanted to be a father to his child? Or relieved that she was willing to walk away without a backwards look if he decided otherwise?

He wasn't sure. None of it made sense yet. Just the very idea that she was in the next room, carrying his baby, sent his brain into a tailspin. And she was right—adding sex back into the mix wasn't going to help that one bit.

He couldn't think straight when he was touching her either. When she kissed him, the rest of the world disappeared and he was focused only on her pleasure. Well, and his.

He wasn't a saint—hell, nobody had ever claimed that about him.

And he had to keep his head on straight right now. All his rules were on the verge of being smashed and he had to figure out how to handle that.

He couldn't let himself get...distracted.

Even if, at the end of this week, he decided to take the risk of being in his child's life, of loving them even knowing he could lose them, that one risk would be all he could manage. Maybe more than he could manage.

He definitely couldn't risk falling for his child's mother too.

And he could, he knew that. Falling for Jenny would be easy—too easy. All it would take was being distracted by the chemistry between them and, before he knew it, his libido would have made choices for his heart that his brain wouldn't back.

She was gorgeous, they had fun together, and the sex was incredible. Yeah, the risk was there.

That was why he'd been so clear about the parameters of their little fling in Iceland from the start. He couldn't let himself sway on those now, even if the situation had changed beyond all recognition.

Jenny was right. There were two options on the table here, and only two.

One: co-parenting with a woman he liked and respected but did not and would not love.

Two: walking away and forgetting this had ever happened.

And right now he still wouldn't risk placing a bet on which side he'd come down on in the end.

It was a damn good job she'd given him a week.

Except…she'd be here. That whole week. Within arm's reach but untouchable.

And Liam already knew that was going to drive him mad.

He heard the click of the shower switching off, and forced himself into action. Somehow, he had to make this week feel perfectly normal. Friendly, even. Not something that was turning his whole world upside down.

He couldn't let on how torn up he was by all this, all the painful memories it dredged up. He'd done his talking in therapy. He'd practised mindfulness and meditation, done the yoga poses and the detoxes. He was living in the goddamn moment now and leaving his past in the past.

And as for the future…well, he'd see about that at the end of the week. It didn't help anybody to plan too far ahead. The universe, in his experience, liked nothing more than upsetting well made plans.

For now, Jenny had to be hungry. She'd been travelling all day, and he'd not even offered her a sandwich before dragging her into the bedroom, so the least he could do was get dinner going.

Or ask someone else to bring it to them, he decided, as a glance inside his fridge forced him to revisit his plans. Grabbing his phone, he fired off a quick email to the housekeeping service he employed, asking them to restock the treehouse with food for two for a week. Then he called his favourite restaurant in the nearest town and sweet-talked Valentina, who owned it, into sending her nephew up to the treehouse on his moped to deliver them some dinner. It wasn't the first time, and he was hoping he could make takeaways a regular offering once the resort was open. They weren't too far away from town to make it feasible.

He'd just hung up when Jenny appeared in the bedroom doorway, dressed in her own clothes again—which was a shame, as Liam had rather enjoyed seeing her in his, but probably for the best considering everything. She was towelling off her damp hair, and there was a tension in the lines of her body that Liam didn't like. It was unfamiliar, the opposite of the relaxation they'd found in each other's company every time they'd been together—until today.

But he knew it wouldn't be going away in a hurry, so he kept his mouth shut.

'I heard you talking to somebody,' she said softly.

'My favourite restaurant,' he replied. 'They're, uh, I asked them to send up some food. I figured you probably wouldn't want to go out tonight, after travelling?' The observation turned into a question as he realised he'd just assumed that would be the case, and not asked her.

But she nodded. 'Yeah. That sounds good. Thanks.'

Crossing the room, she grabbed her suitcase, then stopped. 'Um, I was going to put this away somewhere, but—'

But she didn't know where she was going to sleep. Because they couldn't share the bed any more, could they? And the treehouse only had one bedroom. Damn, he should've known that would come back to bite him eventually. He just hadn't envisioned a situation where someone would come to stay and not want their own space, their own treehouse. Where *he* wouldn't want them to have their own space, away from him.

Except there was no more space, not yet. None of the other treehouses had been finished, and wouldn't be this week. He could call around the hotels down by the beach, but April was the busy season in Costa Rica. Chances of finding her a decent room were slim. And besides, if she was hidden away over there, how would that help him make the decision he needed to make?

'Put it in the bedroom,' he said hurriedly. 'You can take the bed while you're here.'

'And where will you sleep?' Jenny asked.

Liam eyed the squishy sofa for a moment, pitying his poor back, before remembering. 'There's a hammock out on the deck. I used it before the bed was finished. I'll be fine in that for a few nights.'

'If you're sure,' she said, sounding uncertain. 'I could always—'

'Like I'm going to let the pregnant woman sleep in the hammock. Honestly, it's fine.'

'Great. Thanks. Then I'll…' She gestured towards the bedroom and headed off to put away her case.

'There should be some empty drawers under the window,' he called after her.

Maybe, if she took her time unpacking, they wouldn't have to make excruciatingly awkward conversation until the food arrived.

CHAPTER FIVE

NIGHT IN THE rainforest sounded different to night-time anywhere else she'd ever slept.

Not that Jenny was sleeping. That would involve her brain stopping whirring around all the worst-case scenarios it could think of—for this trip, this week, Liam, the baby, her entire future...

It would also require whatever bird was making a racket outside the treehouse going to sleep too. And the crickets, or whatever insect was chirping that way. And what she thought might be frogs.

Liam had warned her that the howler monkeys might wake her up early. Assuming she ever made it to sleep at all. At the moment, it was seeming unlikely.

The worst of it was knowing that he was just outside, lying in that stupid hammock on the deck that surrounded the treehouse, hopefully with some sort of protection against bugs or he'd be miserable in the morning. She had the screened windows, plus the insect repellent body lotion she'd bought before travelling, *and* a net over the bed. What did he have?

Was he out there right now getting eaten alive by mosquitos? Should she check?

She got one foot out of the bed before she caught herself and stopped. Liam had been out here for weeks. His on-site knowledge of the risks had to be more complete than her internet research back in LA. He'd be fine.

And if she went out there now, in the middle of the night, he might get ideas.

Because she sure as hell was having some.

Jenny sighed, turned over, and tried to get more comfortable in the wide, soft, perfectly comfortable and luxurious bed.

Okay, fine. It wasn't the bed. Or the insects and rainforest noises.

It was the scent of Liam on the bedsheets that was keeping her awake.

The reminder of what they'd done there that afternoon. Of what they could do again, if she hadn't put her stupid 'no sex until we make a decision' rule in place.

Giving up on sleep, she sat up in the bed, reached to turn on the light—then stopped. She didn't want to advertise that she was still awake to Liam or to the bugs.

Because it *wasn't* a stupid rule, not really. It was a necessary one.

Jenny had let herself be led around by her libido before, when she was younger and stupider, and she wasn't about to make that mistake again. She wasn't sure how much more she could stand to lose if this all went to hell.

It was just the hormones, anyway. Pregnancy hormones were notorious for making women more sexually charged than normal, weren't they? Although personally sex had been the furthest thing from her mind until she'd seen Liam again.

And then when she had…

Jenny swallowed and reached for her water bottle—only to find it empty. Great. Well, at least she had an excuse to get up. And maybe a small wander around the treehouse would help her settle back to sleep again afterwards. Perhaps there might even be some leftovers of the delicious food Liam had ordered for their dinner. She couldn't help but feel that her enjoyment of the meal had been somewhat thwarted by the tension that filled the room as they ate.

She padded through to the main living area of the treehouse, easing the bedroom door open as silently as she could, and propping it open with the doorstop to avoid it banging closed again. Using her phone as a torch, she refilled her water bottle, then turned to the fridge, where they'd stacked the leftovers. The light from inside the fridge was far brighter than her phone, so she placed it on the counter as she surveyed the takeaway containers.

'Is everything all right?'

Jenny jumped at the sound of Liam's voice behind her, so violently she almost hit her head on the top of the fridge. While she waited for her heart rate to return to something approaching normal, she turned to find him standing on the other side of the kitchen counter.

At least he wasn't topless this time; instead he was wearing a loose cotton top and pyjama bottoms—presumably as a deterrent to the bugs, or in respect for anybody passing through this part of the rainforest, since she knew from personal experience that he usually slept naked.

'I just wanted to get some water.' She motioned towards the now filled water bottle on the counter.

In the light of the fridge door, she saw him raise an eyebrow. Dammit. She should have shut the fridge, except then she wouldn't have been able to see him at all, and that would have been even more alarming.

'And I thought I'd check on the leftovers from dinner,' she admitted.

'Of course. How are they doing?' he asked with a grin. 'Coping okay with fridge life?'

'They look a little forlorn, to be honest.' She returned his smile. 'Like they're not quite fulfilling their life's purpose.'

'Well, we should probably see what we can do about that then, shouldn't we?'

Jenny nodded sagely. 'We should. You get the plates and cutlery. I'll get the food out.'

By unspoken agreement, they left most of the lights dimmed, only turning on one of the lamps in the sitting area for enough light to eat by. She carried the takeout containers over to the low coffee table and they sat on cushions on the floor, safely separated by the heavy wood of the table, as they ate.

It was nice, she realised, halfway through a mouthful of cold empanada. This was the sort of companionship they'd had in Iceland, in between bouts in the bedroom. She'd worried they'd lost it completely, after she'd broken the news about the baby.

But it seemed it was still there. Even if it might only come out under the cover of darkness—and takeout food.

Maybe this was what they needed this week for, more than anything. To find a way to be friends. If Liam decided he wanted to be a part of this, they'd need to be friends—or at least friendly and civil—to co-parent successfully, wouldn't they? That was what the book she'd read on the plane in preparation had said, anyway.

She watched him across the table, darkly handsome in the half light, and felt that familiar heat curl in her belly just at the sight of him. Was it her imagination, or did his eyes darken too? While it was reassuring to know that she wasn't the only one struggling with this issue, it didn't make it any easier to resist either.

He smiled, and her insides flipped again.

Oh, this week was going to be *unbearable*.

This tension between them was going to be the death of him, Liam was certain. It seemed like they could only exist as strangers or lovers, and finding any middle ground was impossible.

. But they were going to have to, if they were to even entertain this co-parenting possibility.

Maybe that was what they needed this week for most of all—a way to figure out how to *be* together without, well, being together.

Or stripping those light, loose cotton pyjamas from her shoulders and exposing all that bare skin he'd had his hands and mouth on so very recently…

Focus, Liam.

Right. Coexisting without sex. That was the plan here.

He tore his gaze away from her own heated one, ignoring the want he saw there. He knew how she felt. But he also knew what she'd said, and there was nothing to do but respect that.

He cast around the room, looking for something—anything—to start a non-sexual conversation about, and finding it harder than he'd imagined. His treehouse retreat wasn't exactly designed as a love nest—more a private escape. But he'd filled it with the textures and items he loved, and everything—from the soft sofas he wanted to lower her onto with his kisses to the solid wood table he couldn't help but imagine laying her on as he took her—made him think of sex.

Maybe it wasn't the treehouse. Maybe it was just him. Or her.

Luckily, Jenny took the conversational thread in hand.

'This food is amazing. Thanks for getting it. I couldn't have faced going out tonight—and if we had, we wouldn't have had leftovers.'

'And the leftovers are the best bit,' Liam replied.

She beamed at him and reached for another helping of the rice with chicken and beans. 'Exactly! I think I'm still making up for not wanting to eat much in the first trimester due to nausea.' She took another empanada and placed it on the edge of her already full plate.

But Liam had frozen, his fork halfway to his mouth. When she gave him a funny look across the coffee table he forced himself to complete the movement. Fork to mouth. Open mouth. Chew food. Swallow. Each step needed a conscious thought—and none of them did anything to distract him from the other thought ricocheting around his head.

'What?' Jenny asked after a long moment. 'You don't want to hear about morning sickness?'

'No!' Liam said hurriedly. He didn't like that resigned tone in her voice. The feeling that he was living down to all her worst expectations of how he was going to react to her news.

He was pretty sure he'd done that already. No need to make it worse.

'Then what?' She raised her eyebrows quizzically at him. 'You looked like I'd just started talking about our sex life in front of your parents.'

Her comparison surprised a laugh out of him, not least because in that instant he could absolutely imagine her sitting at that old farmhouse kitchen table back home in England, telling his mostly deaf father all about that time with the ice cubes and the hot chocolate, while Dad nodded along sagely without hearing a word.

'What *now*?' she asked with a laugh. 'Your face went really weird that time.'

He told her, and she laughed even harder—then sobered up suddenly. 'I guess that's something else we'll need to consider. What you want to tell people—your family and such.'

'One step at a time,' Liam replied, mentally shuffling back from the reminder of his parents, and the fact he hadn't called them in almost a month. The news that he was going to be a father—if that was what he chose to do, at the end of the week—wasn't something that could be shared by phone, anyway. His mother would never forgive him if he wasn't there to be hugged the moment he told her. Jenny too, for that matter. Would she come to England with him to tell them? Or would that be beyond the constraints of their co-parenting agreement?

Too much. Too fast. Too deep.

He picked up another forkful of food and returned to intense focus on chewing and swallowing. Far safer than trying to picture a future that might never happen.

'So, what was it that freaked you out?' Jenny asked. 'If it wasn't the morning sickness thing. What did I say?'

'It was just…the first time you really spoke about the fact that our baby is inside you right now, and it felt…real.' Not a possible future, but something that was happening right now, in this room with him.

He knew intellectually, of course, that babies didn't just spring forth fully grown without any preparation. He knew that Jenny was pregnant. He just hadn't really imagined that the child could already be affecting the world it wasn't even part of yet, that was all.

Jenny gave him a small understanding smile. 'I think I get what you mean. I mean, I'm not even showing yet, but I can definitely feel the changes in my body. But no one else can. It's like…it almost didn't feel real because nobody else knew, and then I'd feel a wave of nausea, or my boobs would hurt, and I'd know it *was* real. Just still secret.'

Liam frowned. '*No one* else knew? You haven't told *anybody* but me? Not even Winter?'

'Just you.' She met his gaze with her own clear, honest one. 'I figured you had a right to know first.'

It was a perfectly natural decision. But somehow Liam doubted that was the real reason she'd made it.

He could understand not telling Winter, because her boss had her own issues with pregnancy that made it complicated. But not telling *anyone* else?

Liam couldn't help wondering if that was because she didn't have anyone else to tell.

What about her family? He thought again about his own. Were her family still around? What was her relationship with them? This was all stuff he was going to need to know eventually, if he went ahead with this.

His carefully curated small circle of people that mattered would have to grow, one way or another.

'Besides,' Jenny went on, nibbling on the edge of an empanada, 'they say not to tell people until after the twelve-week scan. Just in case.'

Just in case. He knew what that meant. He'd never spent a lot of time around babies or pregnant women—certainly not in the last five years—but that rule he remembered.

Julie had never made it to her twelve-week scan. She'd lost her life, and the baby's, in the accident, two weeks before they had it scheduled.

But before that she'd been adamant they not tell people too. Just in case.

Besides, I like having a secret that's just

ours, she'd whispered to him late at night, when the horizon was already a little fuzzy from the beer and whisky he'd consumed before, during and after their dinner. Julie's eyes were clear, though—she'd stopped drinking the moment she saw that positive test. Smoking too.

She'd done everything right. Which was how he knew her death, their baby's death, was his fault.

Liam shook away the memory. 'And when is the twelve-week scan?' His chest felt tight just asking the question. If she said two weeks' time...but wait, if the baby had been conceived in Iceland... He tried to do the maths in his head, but the weeks had merged into one a bit since he'd arrived in Costa Rica. And wasn't there something about the dating going from *before* the sex? He was sure he remembered something about that, if only because it made no sense at all.

'Oh.' Jenny looked down at her almost empty plate. 'Um... Actually, I already had it. Before I came. I wanted to be sure...'

She trailed off, but he knew what she meant. She'd wanted to be sure the baby was okay. That the pregnancy was real, and viable. That this was really happening. She'd wanted to be sure before she'd told him, because otherwise what was the point in seeking him out at all?

Not that he'd been under any illusion that she'd have come all this way if it hadn't been for the baby, but still the thought stung anyway.

Was it that if she'd miscarried, or the scan had shown something bad, he might never have known he'd lost out on being a father again? He forced himself to focus on what he was feeling—something every retreat he'd ever been on had assured him was important, and something he avoided doing unless absolutely necessary.

It seemed necessary now.

No, he realised. He wasn't angry, or even annoyed or frustrated at her revelation.

He was...disappointed. A little sad that he'd missed out on that moment again—sharing that moment with her.

And, more than anything, he felt guilty that she'd had to do that alone. That she hadn't wanted to ask him—or anyone else—to be there with her.

He was starting to get the impression that,

despite her bubbly nature, her confidence and her obviously good relationship with her boss, Jenny didn't have a lot of people in her life that she could trust.

He didn't know yet if he was capable of being one. But he couldn't dismiss the feeling that he *wanted* to be.

Liam swallowed, keeping the emotion down inside where it belonged.

'Are there…did you get pictures?'

Jenny beamed at his question. 'I did. Do you want to see?'

He nodded, and tried to ignore the sensation of falling deeper into something he wasn't sure he had the strength to climb out of again.

CHAPTER SIX

JENNY WAS SURPRISED by how well she slept after her midnight feast with Liam—at least, after she'd taken her indigestion medication, anyway. Pregnancy was just hell on the digestive system. Still, she woke up feeling more relaxed and refreshed than she had in weeks—something she assigned to having finally shared the giant secret that had consumed her life ever since she'd peed on that stick.

He'd seemed surprised that she hadn't told anyone else. But really, who was she going to tell?

Winter would be the obvious person, she supposed. More friend than boss after so many years, the A-list actress and director was definitely the person Jenny spent the most time with these days.

But Winter had experienced her own preg-

nancy issues, and they'd left scars. Jenny
hadn't wanted to burden her with the knowledge. Add in the fact that she was so recently
reunited with her ex-husband, Josh, and Winter had enough going on in her life without
worrying about Jenny's too.

The fact that Josh was Liam's best friend,
and that the two of them would definitely
have Opinions about his knocking her up,
might have played into that decision.

And apart from Winter...there really
wasn't anyone else she *would* tell. Her job
took her all over the world, gave her oppor-
tunities and experiences she'd never have had
otherwise, and it fulfilled her in ways she'd
never expected when Winter first hired her.
But it didn't leave a lot of downtime for making friends who'd be excited to hear her news.

As for her family...well. She'd just have
to hope that Liam's family would be excited
enough for both of them, because she had no
intention of even letting hers know what had
happened.

Since her grandma had passed away, Jenny
found it easier to believe that she simply
didn't *have* a family any more. They'd made
it clear that was what they wanted, anyway.

She'd always believed, growing up, that family were the people who loved you, looked after you and supported you even when the rest of the world turned against you. She knew now, though, that had been the naïve understanding of a child.

She'd made one mistake— she'd fallen in love with the wrong man—and her whole life had unravelled. And instead of being there to help her rebuild, to tell her that she was still loved, that there was no mistake she could make that would ever change that…

Her family had asked her to leave. Told her that she was a disgrace. That her actions were ruining their lives.

Grandma had been the only one who'd felt different, but she'd died just a few months later.

And since then… Well. Jenny knew now that family didn't mean love any more than sex did. And neither of them were something you could trust enough to build a future on.

No, she wasn't going to tell her family. She wouldn't give them the chance to turn away from her child the way they'd turned away from her.

So, Liam was it, at least for now. Once she

knew what level of involvement he wanted, and how they were going to make things work, *then* she could talk to Winter and start figuring things out. She was under no illusion that life would be able to remain the same once she had a baby. But she hoped in that future she would be able to hold onto the things she loved most about her life.

Maybe she could build an even better one than the one she'd been living for the last few years. With or without Liam's help.

She heard the screen door of the treehouse open, and realised Liam must be awake too. Time to get up.

She showered quickly and dressed in a T-shirt and a pair of shorts that were suddenly beginning to get a little tight around the waist, as if her body felt that now the secret was out it could start changing in earnest. Or maybe she was just bloated after her midnight feast. Her body was a mystery to her.

As she entered the living area, Liam looked up from where he sat at the kitchen bar and smiled, before nodding to the coffee pot. Then he turned back to whatever he was reading on his tablet.

Jenny weighed up the option of the coffee.

She could tell by the aroma that it was thick and strong and dark, and it made her mouth water. But her doctor had been adamant that she was only allowed a certain amount of caffeine a day during her pregnancy, and she was pretty sure that one cup from Liam's pot would take her over her limit immediately.

Would she regret it later if she drank the coffee now? Trying to predict the future was a difficult and often fruitless task, but she didn't need Grandma's Tarot cards to tell her that, come her usual after lunch slump, she'd regret having used up her caffeine allowance so early.

Instead, she rifled around in the cupboards and found some fruit teas and made herself a cup of that instead, only glancing wistfully at the coffee pot a few times.

Liam pulled out pastries and fruit and breads for breakfast, and they ate in companionable silence—him engrossed in whatever he was reading and she watching him. They'd never had breakfast together, she realised, not really. Most nights they'd spent together in Iceland she'd crept back to the suite she was sharing with Winter, so her absence wouldn't be noted and commented on endlessly in the morning.

She wasn't completely surprised to discover that Liam wasn't much of a morning person.

'Sorry,' he said, after draining his second cup of coffee—not that she was bitterly counting or anything—and putting aside his tablet. 'I'm not much for conversation before my second cup of the day.'

'I noticed,' she said with a smile. 'So, now you're fully conscious…any plans for the day?'

He nodded and reached for another slice of watermelon. 'Actually, yes. I had a thought last night. If we're going to make any of this work at all, we need to figure out a way to be friends. Starting with learning a little more about each other.'

Jenny felt her shoulder muscles stiffen automatically and worked to relax them. 'Getting to know each other' always led to the sort of awkward questions she didn't want to answer, in her experience. But on the other hand she had to admit she'd followed a similar train of thought the night before too.

They needed to get to know each other if they were even going to consider co-parenting. But that didn't have to mean opening up about her past, her family, or any of that, did it? All Liam really needed to know was who she was *now,* and the sort of mother she'd be to their child.

She didn't have to tell him anything she wasn't ready for him to know. And she definitely wasn't ready to confess all about her past. She knew how he'd look at her if he knew—either the same way people had at the time, when the story hit the papers and online, with disgust and disappointment. Or, if she was lucky, pity—for the naivety that had led her into that situation in the first place.

She'd had more than enough of both those reactions at the time, and she didn't want to see *either* of them on Liam's face.

But it *would* be good to learn a little more about the enigma that was Liam Delaney— especially if he was going to be part of her and her child's life. Which meant giving up some stuff of her own, she supposed.

As long as she got to control how much.

So she nodded. 'I suppose there's probably more to learn about you than what you like in bed and that you're kinda bad at mornings.' Dammit. She really hadn't meant to say that.

His answering smirk told her that his brain had gone to the same place hers had, and for a long moment he held her gaze trapped in his own, imagining all the things they weren't saying. Or doing.

Nope. No sex. That's the rule. If I can't have coffee, I sure as hell can't have sex with this man either. It's far more dangerous.

Liam broke first and looked away, gathering up his breakfast things and carrying them to the sink, and the moment was over.

'So. You had a plan?' She reached for her fruit tea and tried not to wince at the taste.

'I thought I'd show you around a bit. Take you down to the beach, have lunch at my favourite café, that sort of thing.'

He reached over to take her plate too and began stacking the dishwasher. She suspected he probably had a housekeeping service who'd have done that for him while they were out, so maybe it was just a displacement activity. She could appreciate the need for that. And it was kind of…nice to see him doing something so domestic. Something she could imagine a father doing.

Not that he was on board with that yet.

'That sounds lovely.' She had to admit,

after all the drama of yesterday—not to mention the travel, and the midnight snack—she was a little drained today, despite sleeping well.

'And we can talk,' Liam added. She wasn't entirely sure if she just imagined the ominous tone in his voice.

'I'll go get ready.' Jenny hopped off her stool and headed for the bedroom, her mind already whirring.

If Liam wanted to Talk, she was going to make sure she had her own stack of awkward questions to pose for every one he asked her.

He might be right that the only way to make a decision about their future was to open up and understand each other. But that didn't mean it wasn't going to be utter torture getting there. And she sure as hell wouldn't be the only one going through that.

The beach closest to the resort was one of Liam's favourite places in the world—and Jenny seemed charmed by it too. He'd discovered it almost by accident when exploring the proposed resort site and known instantly that he was in the right place.

'What's this place called?' Jenny had her

sandals in her hand as they walked along the pale white sand. Beside them, the waves sparkled bright blue in the sunshine. There were a few intrepid surfers out there but it was still early, and few people not staying very locally would have made their way down the twisty jungle path to reach this particular beach yet—not when there were so many others nearby to enjoy.

The rainforest curled around both edges of the sand, giving the cove a secluded, protected feeling. There were no large resorts built up to the edge of the sand here—only a small, ramshackle café at the far end, owned by the sister-in-law of Valentina, who ran the companion restaurant in town. It always looked like it was about to fall down, but the food was every bit as good as the more polished town restaurant—maybe even better. Not that he planned to tell Valentina that.

Liam liked to think that this beach would almost be a secret, just for people staying in his treehouses, and a few others in the know. A special, private place without the crowds or the noise of some of the larger, better-known beaches.

'I wasn't sure it even had a name for ages,'

he admitted. 'But then I heard one of the locals call it Playa Escondida—which means Hidden Beach, I think. So that's what I call it too.'

'It suits it.' She paused on the sand, turning a slow circle to take in all the views. Liam smiled as he watched her, something in him just glad that she found the same magic in this place that he did.

He'd built retreat hotels all over the world, always seeking out special places where his guests could rest, recharge, and check out of the real world for a while until they were ready to face reality again. From the Californian desert to the volcanic landscape and geothermal pools of Iceland, he built places outside time.

He was proud of all his retreats, but he just knew that his Costa Rican treehouse resort was going to be the most special of all.

Even Jenny was falling for it, he could tell. He watched her turn, her expression more relaxed than it had been since she'd arrived, her blonde hair glowing in the sunlight.

God, he wanted to kiss her. He wanted to wrap her up in his arms and kiss her here, barefoot on this beach, the waves shining behind them, like the end of one of those rom-com movies he used to star in.

What the hell was wrong with him?

It's just lust, he reassured himself. After all, being told he couldn't have something had always made him want it more.

But he wouldn't give in to that desire, even if Jenny indicated for a moment that she wanted him to. She'd regret it later, he knew, and he wouldn't do that to her.

Not until they'd made a decision about the future, anyway.

Jenny stopped twirling suddenly and froze, staring across the beach to the closest point where it became jungle. Liam followed her gaze, and grinned when he realised what had caught her attention.

'Is that a sloth?' she asked, her voice filled with incredulity.

'It is.' The slow-moving creature loped unhurriedly across the rainforest floor, right beside the sand, before starting to shimmy up the next tree. 'You're lucky to see one down on the ground; they only come down from the trees about once a week. But if you look up when we're in the jungle, you'll likely see a whole lot more.'

'This place is amazing.' The sloth disappeared into the tree canopy, and Jenny turned to him with a blinding smile that made his whole body tighten in response. 'So, what wonders do you have for me next?'

They took their time exploring their way along the beach, watching the few surfers tackling the waves, and observing a small snorkelling lesson taking off from a boat. They didn't see any more sloths, but they heard macaws overhead, and what might have been a monkey scampering through the trees as they approached the café.

Liam knew they were supposed to be spending this time getting to know each other, but it was hard to pull the conversation from the wonders around them to their personal histories and issues—especially when so much of his concentration had to go into keeping his distance from her. It would be so easy to just reach out and touch the small of her back as he guided her along their path, or to grab her hand to show her something interesting. Or even to catch her in his arms when she lost her footing on the soft sand and hold her close against him…

No. Not doing that.

Instead, he attempted occasional questions about how she came to live in LA, or her family, her childhood, but each time Jenny deflected them with an observation about their surroundings.

He was beginning to wonder if she wanted to hide from her own past as much as he did his.

Eventually, however, they reached the end of the beach—and Isabela's café. 'Come on,' he said, when she looked dubiously at the structure. 'I promised you lunch.'

Isabela bustled over to greet them the moment the door banged shut. Inside, the beach café was cool and shady, and even Liam felt it a welcome relief from the April heat—Jenny sighed blissfully beside him, and he realised he probably should have got her out of the sun sooner.

They were shown to the best table, such as it was—a rickety wooden thing set for two, away from the long bar where one or two locals sat and eyed them suspiciously, and beside the open windows where they could watch the activity on the beach, and the waves washing in and out.

With Jenny's permission, he ordered for

both of them, asking Isabela in Spanish to just bring them whatever was best today. He'd eaten there enough to trust her judgement.

Isabela's teenage son brought them iced water and then, when they declined beer, some fruit juice Liam's taste buds couldn't quite identify.

'So, in the interests of getting to know one another,' Liam said when they were alone again. 'Is this your first time in South America?'

The tension that had appeared in her expression at his first statement faded a little, and she nodded. 'Never been further south than Florida before. But then, Florida's a long way from Canada, where I grew up. And even further from…where is it, exactly, you're from?'

'England,' he replied succinctly. 'In case the accent wasn't a giveaway.'

She rolled her eyes. 'I know that much. *Where* in England?'

'Norfolk. But you could have found that much out from Wikipedia.'

She flashed him a smile. 'I do have a bit of an advantage there,' she admitted. 'Your whole life is laid out on the internet by intrepid fans.'

Had she looked him up? Probably. It was hard not to, when the information was just sitting there. He'd idly googled other actors just while watching them in a movie—it was unrealistic to believe that Jenny wouldn't have looked up the man who'd fathered her child.

Which meant she must already know the answers to the questions she was asking. So why ask them? Unless it was to stop him asking deeper, more personal ones of her.

There was something guarded in her eyes, something brittle in her smile, and he suddenly wondered what he *would* find if he ran an internet search for Jenny Bouchard. Because nobody could avoid their life being documented on the internet any more, could they? It was always all there if a person knew where to look.

He knew where to look. He could do a little research after she went to bed tonight and find out all there was to know about the secrets Jenny Bouchard was keeping, he was sure.

But he'd rather she trust him enough to tell him herself.

'What?' Jenny asked, and he realised he'd been staring at her for long moments.

Liam shook his head. 'Nothing. Look, here comes our food. I promise you you're going to love this.'

He could be patient. He had time. Well, he had a week.

She'd tell him her secrets before that week was out.

CHAPTER SEVEN

COSTA RICA WAS so much more beautiful and amazing than Jenny had imagined, but she still returned to the treehouse that night feeling like she'd dodged a bullet. After their—admittedly delicious—lunch of local fare served tapas style, she'd expected Liam to start up his promised questioning in earnest.

But he hadn't.

Instead, he'd stuck to the general getting-to-know-a-person questions that had no hidden traps. She'd expected, at the least, a bit of a quiz about her family in Canada, and why she'd left, but as if he had a second sense for the sort of questions that would make her clam up, he'd avoided any mention of family at all, after his first couple of attempts on the beach.

He'd kept asking questions, though, all through their trip back to the treehouse, the simple dinner he'd cooked for her from the magically stocked fridge, right up until she started yawning and he sent her to bed and retreated to his hammock.

So now he knew her favourite colour—green—her favourite movie, her teenage crush, the most insane thing she'd ever seen on a publicity tour with Winter, that she only liked salted popcorn, not sweet, and a dozen other meaningless facts—but he still had no idea why she hadn't spoken to her parents in over five years, or why she'd moved to LA and started working for Winter in the first place.

Which was a good thing, she reminded herself when she woke up still thinking about it the next morning. She didn't *want* to tell him those things.

But it did make her feel a little guilty.

She knew that she couldn't possibly expect to raise a child with a man she couldn't be honest with, one she couldn't trust with the basic details of her past. But trust…that was a sticky word for her these days. She'd trusted her family. She'd trusted Anthony.

And look where all that trust had got her.

But this situation was different. She wasn't

expecting Liam to love her. The point remained, though. If they were going to do this together, she couldn't hide from the truth. She'd have to tell him everything eventually.

Just not yet.

Of course there was still the strong chance that he was going to walk away at the end of the week and then there'd never be any need to tell him...

Except that wasn't fair either. He needed all the information to be able to make the decision about his future in the first place. It was no less than she'd expect.

Whatever the outcome of this week, it had to be based on a foundation of honest truth. There couldn't be any room left for what-ifs and wrong decisions.

Not having all the information, or at least not the *true* information, from Anthony was part of what had led her down that road to disaster last time. She expected the truth from Liam, which meant she had to give it in return.

She just might need a little time to build up to it.

He, on the other hand, didn't have that

choice—of waiting to tell her his secrets in his own time.

Because *of course* she'd googled him to find out all she could about him, before she came down to Costa Rica to tell him he was going to be a father. Who wouldn't?

So she knew about his parents' farm in Norfolk, how it had been about to go under until he'd saved it with the fee from his first big Hollywood movie. She knew he was the youngest of the family, with three older sisters. She could list the films he'd made, the co-stars he'd dated. She'd read all the old reports about his wild child ways, seen the photos of him staggering out of nightclubs with a blonde on his arm.

She'd read the interviews he'd given during those years—and noticed that he hadn't given one in the last five years.

And she knew why.

Even before she'd met him in Iceland, she'd known that much. Everybody in LA did. She remembered it happening, her first full month in LA.

Liam and his actress girlfriend at the time, Julie Oswald, had been at a party at some director's house in the Hollywood Hills. It was a big deal, lots of stars there, and lots of alcohol and drugs, by all accounts.

When they'd left in the early hours Julie had been driving. And, according to the inquest, she'd accidentally driven them through a red light and been hit by a car coming the other way that hit the driver's side. Julie had been killed on impact and Liam…

Liam, on the other side of the car, had survived. With, it seemed, miraculously few injuries.

At least, not physical ones.

Winter and Josh, two of Liam's closest friends even back then, didn't talk about what had happened next—and Jenny hadn't known how to ask without sounding like she was prying, which she would have been, and inviting questions she didn't want to answer about why it mattered to her anyway.

She wondered, though, as she watched him over breakfast, about the non-visible injuries. The ones that had changed the very person he was from the inside out, because of what had happened.

Jenny knew about that sort of injury, even though she'd never been in an accident half as traumatic as the one Liam had lived through.

Maybe those were the secrets she still needed to hear from Liam before this week was up. Maybe those secrets would be worth sharing her own for.

Starting from a place of total honesty.

What a novel idea for a relationship.

Probably only a possibility because this *wasn't* a relationship. Nobody in a relationship ever told the whole truth, did they? Otherwise the US divorce rate would be even higher.

'So, what's the plan for today?' she asked as he drained the dregs of his second cup of coffee.

'I thought I'd take you further up the coast a way, to another retreat of sorts,' he said. 'A friend of mine runs a yoga studio there and has a pregnancy yoga class this morning.'

Jenny blinked. 'You're taking me to pregnancy yoga?' Wasn't that the sort of thing that besotted, doting husbands and boyfriends did? Not casual flings who weren't even sure they wanted to be part of their kid's life.

Liam gave an uncomfortable shrug. 'Honestly, I needed to go up there this week anyway. We're negotiating her bringing her studio in under my resort banner and running sessions here for guests. It just so happens that she has a pregnancy class today.'

'Right. Of course.' That made more sense. Basically, he was finding a way to keep his business running while she was here. She couldn't complain about that.

'We might see some more sloths or monkeys, though,' he added, and she couldn't help but smile at the idea.

Not least because if they were admiring the wildlife they wouldn't be baring their souls to each other.

The roads they travelled on were twisty, uneven and often barely worthy of the name, but Liam's four-by-four took the sharp corners and dips without much complaint. Jenny stared at his tanned, toned forearms, the muscles there cording as he turned the wheel, and couldn't help but remember how it felt to have those arms around her.

She looked away.

Not thinking about that. Not thinking about him that way.

That was easier said than done, though. Even as she stared out of the window instead, memories of the dreams that had plagued her sleep filled her head instead.

Dreams where she wasn't alone in that big bed in the treehouse. Where Liam's body was curled behind her, his mouth at her neck, his hand at her breast, his hardness pressed up against her.

The way his hand drifted down her body. The way she parted her legs to let him in…

She cleared her throat and turned her attention back to the car. Maybe she should turn the air-con up a bit.

'You're a good driver,' she said after he navigated another particularly tricky section of road.

He shrugged but didn't answer. Too late, she realised that it might be a sensitive subject, given his history, even if he *hadn't* been driving the night of the accident.

They drove in silence for a few more minutes. Jenny went back to scanning the trees around her for wildlife, but couldn't spot any. She was about to start counting trees to distract her from the memories of her dreams when Liam spoke again.

'So, next question.'

'You didn't ask enough yesterday?'

'Not by half.' There was something in his voice, a steely hardness, that told her he was done going easy on her. Which meant she couldn't afford to go easy on him either.

If he wanted her secrets, he'd have to give up his own in return. That much she knew for certain.

'How did you come to work for Winter?' he asked.

She considered her answer. On the one hand, the full story gave away every humiliating, soul-destroying detail of the worst six months of her life.

But it didn't have to. Not if she told it right.

She wasn't ready to tell him everything just yet. She would, she promised herself. But she needed to work up to it.

And in the meantime she could give him *something,* couldn't she?

'I wanted to be an actress,' she said, keeping her tone breezy and her gaze away from his. 'So I moved from Canada to LA, and started looking for work.' She shrugged, as if a little embarrassed not to have made it in the notoriously difficult industry. 'When that didn't happen, I figured working for a star was better than waiting tables. I joined a recruitment agency, and they got me the interview. I had good office experience, I'm proactive, and Winter and I hit it off when we met. It was as simple as that.'

She'd expected it to be harder, but Winter had been determined and wasn't into wasting time. She couldn't have known then, she mused, how much that one interview would change her life.

'And you like working for her?'

'Very much. She's more of a friend than an employer these days.'

'But you still haven't told her about the baby.' Liam glanced across at her for a brief moment, before returning his attention to the road. 'You'll have to, though. Especially if you want to keep working for her.'

'I do,' she said quickly. The last thing she needed was Liam getting any ideas about her giving up her life and her dreams to follow him around the planet with a baby in tow. 'And we'll figure it out somehow. Once I know what *your* expectations are in all this.'

It didn't hurt to remind him that it wasn't her holding up the ability to make plans for the future here.

'Right. I'm sure you will.' She listened hard for any sarcasm in his voice, but she didn't find it.

'Your turn,' she said, already formulating her question in her mind. She didn't want to ask about the accident, not straight off. But there was something she'd always wanted to know… 'Do you think you'll ever go back to acting?'

'No.' His answer was fast, firm and didn't leave a lot of room for follow-up questions. But she asked one anyway.

'Why not?'

'There's nothing left there for me.'

She stared at the bleak expression on his face, the absolute certainty that anything about that part of his life was over, and knew that the papers and the internet only had half the story.

They said Liam Delaney had walked away from that car accident with only minor injuries.

But they were wrong.

'We're here,' Liam said as they took a final turn and suddenly a small wooden complex tucked in between the trees came into view. 'There's Selena, my yoga teacher friend.' He nodded towards the terrace, where a gorgeous dark-haired, tanned and toned woman in a loose shirt and tight shorts stood, smiling widely and waving.

Of course. Of course Liam's friend was gorgeous. She probably glistened rather than perspired too, like all the yoga gurus on YouTube, while Jenny would be sweating like a pig in no time.

Good job they'd taken sex off the table, really.

Jenny seemed a little reticent when he dumped her on Selena with barely a hello and goodbye, apart from the warm welcome hug Selena always insisted on. He'd planned to stay and show Jenny round a bit, maybe even watch some of the yoga session. But after her questions in the car...he needed some space.

And luckily there was always the excuse of work, of conversations he needed to have to keep building up the new resort, to keep him busy and distracted.

Distraction was definitely what he needed today. As if Jenny in her tight yoga gear, showing off every curve he wasn't allowed to touch, wasn't enough, then there were the questions.

Do you think you'll ever go back to acting?

Not if they paid him. Which they would, of course. A lot. But it didn't matter.

He wasn't that person any more, and he never wanted to be him again.

That thought gave him pause, as he considered the only question that really mattered this week. What would the old Liam do about the baby? Maybe if he knew that, he could do the opposite. It was what he'd done in almost every other area of his life.

Old Liam had been excited about Julie's pregnancy. He'd been gung-ho about parenthood, proud of his ability to father a child and naively confident that everything would work out fine, one way or another.

If they'd lived…

He slumped against the railing outside the yoga studio as the realisation hit him.

If they'd lived, he'd have been a terrible father. He'd have handed off responsibility to Julie, or the nannies they'd inevitably hire. He'd have breezed in between shoots and parties to do the fun stuff, sure, but he wouldn't have been involved—not the way his own parents had been. He hadn't had that in him then, too caught up in his own success, his own demons, and the lifestyle both afforded him.

Liam wasn't proud of the man he'd been back then. After leaving home and finding such easy success…he'd grown selfish, entitled even. Focused on finding greater success—or notoriety.

The accident had stolen that life from him—taken so many things he'd never recover from the loss of—but it had given him something in return: a new perspective on his own existence.

He was a different man now, because of the accident, and what followed. Whatever the old him would have done, he could do different. Better.

But did that mean he should settle down and raise a child? That this was his second chance? Or that he *shouldn't* be excited about the baby at all? What was the opposite action to the one he'd have taken then?

Was it responsibly stepping away, giving Jenny financial support but not getting involved emotionally? Because while he'd changed beyond recognition, one thing hadn't.

He wasn't going to be able to stay still and be a doting dad, the way his own had been. Growing up on the farm, his dad had been busy, for sure—farming meant working a lot of hours, and many of them unsociable. But he'd been *there*. If Liam needed him, he'd only had to tag along into the fields after he'd finished his morning chores feeding and cleaning out various animals. His dad would let him follow along until Liam was ready to talk about whatever was on his mind, and then he'd listen. *Really* listen. He'd keep working, and that was good because it meant Liam wouldn't have to look him in the eye while he talked. But he heard every word, because at the end he'd offer Liam the advice he wanted, or the words he needed to hear.

Liam had never once felt worse about himself, or a situation, after talking to his father as a child. He wished he could say the same about the experience as an adult.

He knew what his dad would say. He'd put aside all his disappointment about Liam as a man—his wild past, the way he never came home, his behaviour on the rare occasions he had visited before the accident—and he'd be purely excited at the prospect of another grandchild. He and Mum would welcome Jenny into their family, their home, in a heartbeat.

And if Liam told him he was contemplating *not* being a part of the child's life… he'd never understand.

Which was why he couldn't tell him.

But it didn't take away the fundamental question. How could he be the kind of father his own had been if he was travelling all over the world between his resorts, setting up new sites, and continuing to build the business he loved—the business that had saved him after the accident?

And if he couldn't be the kind of father his kid deserved—would the baby be better off without him anyway?

He didn't find any answers on his tour of the yoga studio grounds, but when he returned to collect Jenny an hour later he found her smiling and glowing from the exercise. Hopefully that meant it had been a good decision to bring her here.

'You enjoyed the class?' he asked as he approached Jenny and Selena.

Jenny nodded. 'Very much. It felt good to stretch my body and feel like it's still mine— even if I'm sharing it right now.'

Sharing it with his child. Liam couldn't help the slight feeling of pride and satisfaction that surged through him as his gaze dropped to her still flat belly.

'It's important to keep that connection with your body,' Selena said with a smile. 'You did great today. Come back any time.'

She hugged Jenny, who looked mildly awkward at the interaction, then stepped away.

'Did you want to try the hot springs before we head back to the treehouse?' Liam asked. 'They're wonderful after a workout.'

'Oh, um…' Jenny darted a glance at Selena, who winced.

'I'm afraid that the hot springs are not recommended for expectant mothers, Liam,' she said apologetically.

'Right. Of course. Sorry.' Should he have known that? Probably. How much else was he supposed to know about pregnancy that he didn't? And how much more about babies and children? *You don't know how much you don't know,* his father used to say. 'I guess we'll head back, then.'

He'd half hoped that Jenny would be too tired to ask more questions on the drive back. But when she did, they weren't the questions he'd expected.

'So, you and Selena,' she said as he drove

away from the yoga studio and hot springs. 'Were you two ever a…well, couple, I guess? Or anything.'

He blinked, then concentrated on the road. 'Me and Selena? No. She's married to Gael, who runs the place with her. He's been helping me out a lot with plans for the resort, and I'm hoping to bring them both in on-site when we open.'

'Oh. Right.' She stared out of the window rather than look at him.

'Were you…jealous?'

'No!' Her response was fast and emphatic—but not entirely convincing.

'Are you sure?' he teased. 'I mean, I'd understand…'

She reached across to lightly hit his thigh, and he grabbed her hand, swallowing at the instant spark he always felt when they touched.

Maybe teasing wasn't a good idea. Not when neither of them was willing to follow up where it might lead.

God knew he wanted to, though. And the idea of Jenny being jealous… It might be juvenile, but he had to admit he didn't hate it. Keeping his hands off her was a challenge, and keeping his thoughts away from how good it could be if they gave in… that was proving impossible. It would be nice to know that she was struggling with the same thing.

'Not jealous.' She snatched her hand away and tucked it under her leg. Almost as if she didn't trust herself not to touch him again.

Liam smiled. 'Of course not.'

'We don't have that kind of relationship, and it's not like we've made any promises to each other—or intend to.'

'Right.' They'd both been clear on that from the start. Neither of them was looking for anything serious or long-term—even if it seemed to have found them anyway. They'd be tied for life now, because of the baby. *If* he chose to be involved.

If he didn't, he would never see her again. He'd have to make sure of that.

If he stepped back she wouldn't want him showing up in her life, just because he was friends with her boss.

'It was just… I realised it was another thing we'll need to deal with. Plan for, even. If we end up doing this parenting thing together.'

'What? Selena and Gael?'

'No. I mean…if we're co-parenting, we'll both have to deal with the other dating other people. Maybe even settling down and getting serious with them. We'd need to agree how that was going to work too.' She sighed. 'There's just…so much. If we do this, we're connected for the rest of our lives.'

'Yeah. I had the same realisation today too.' The weight of it all hung heavy around his neck, threatening to pull him back down.

But down to where? The dark place he'd been after Julie died?

He couldn't risk that. Not even for his child.

He'd worked too hard to find this level of acceptance of the world. To make peace with his past and work towards a new future.

And the idea of watching his child's mother—watching *Jenny*—fall in love with another man…that stirred up emotions he'd kept buried for a long time now. Ones he didn't want to feel again.

But what was the alternative? Stay away completely, of course. But if he wanted to be involved he had to accept that idea of the future. Because of course she'd fall in love with someone—and any man in his right mind would jump at the chance to fall for her.

Unless he was willing to be that man—

He broke off the thought and centred himself, focusing very hard on the road ahead. That wasn't him. He wasn't there yet—and he suspected he never would be.

Love led to loss. And he knew too well that his broken psyche couldn't take any more of that.

They drove the rest of the way home in silence, each lost in their own thoughts. But when they arrived Liam hurried around to the passenger door to help her out, then left his hand on her arm to stall her for a moment.

'What?' She looked up at him, eyes wide and wondering, and the only thing he wanted in the world was to kiss her. To kiss her and never stop.

He looked away and cleared his throat. 'I just… We'll figure it out, okay? Whatever we decide, we'll do it together, and we'll make it work together. Yeah?'

He could see her throat move as she swallowed, her gaze never leaving his. Were the same thoughts flooding her brain that had taken over his? The feeling that what tied them together was more than just the baby growing inside her?

He didn't have the courage to ask.

Finally she nodded. 'Yeah. Together.'

Then, with a tight smile, she brushed past him towards the treehouse stairs. Liam took a moment to steel himself against another evening playing house with a woman he longed to touch but couldn't, then followed.

CHAPTER EIGHT

JENNY BRAVELY RESISTED the coffee again at breakfast the next morning, but when Liam announced his plans to take her to a little coffee roastery café where they could roast their own beans before drinking the strong, heavenly brew, she broke.

'I need to take a meeting with the owner anyway about supplying the resort when we open, so I thought it would be perfect,' he said. 'I remember from Iceland how much you like your coffee.'

'You do realise that pregnant women are supposed to limit their caffeine intake,' she snapped, and regretted losing her temper as he blinked cluelessly at her. 'Have you not noticed that I haven't drunk more than a cup of coffee a day since I got here?'

'Um…actually…no.' He winced. 'Sorry.

I knew about avoiding alcohol, but I didn't think…sorry.'

Jenny's shoulders slumped, and she sighed. 'That's okay. I mean, it's not as if you've spent a lot of time around pregnant women, I suppose.'

Liam looked away. 'No. No, I haven't.'

He looked so distraught at his screw-up that she felt sorry enough for him to let him off the hook. 'Look, you go take your meeting. I'm pretty tired today anyway. I'll hang out here, enjoy the rainforest. Take a nap. That sort of thing.'

'Are you sure?' he asked. 'I won't be long. But there's stuff in the fridge for lunch when you get hungry. And I'll take you out for dinner to make it up to you.'

'It's a deal,' she said with a smile.

She'd expected to feel relief when he was gone. The past few days in each other's constant company in a rather small treehouse had been kind of intense—not to mention the moment yesterday by the car when she'd been *sure* he was about to kiss her. It was all getting a bit much, and she'd actually felt a little lighter at the idea of a reprieve. Of not spending every moment reminding herself why she couldn't just reach over and touch him, kiss him. Couldn't give in to the chemistry that still simmered between them, all the damn time.

She needed just a couple of hours to be by herself with her thoughts and figure out how she felt about everything.

But strangely, the moment he was gone, she just found that she missed his company.

It made sense in a way, she reasoned as she took a long, not too hot shower. When Liam was around she wasn't alone in this pregnancy. She wasn't solely responsible for the life growing inside her.

But he wouldn't always be around. Even if he decided to be part of this, they weren't going to be doing it as a couple. Their conversation about other partners in the car had only made that clearer.

So sometimes she *would* be alone. She would have to learn to do this by herself. Just like everything else in her life over the last five years.

I knew that. I came here knowing I'd probably be doing this on my own.

But somewhere between shower sex and pregnancy yoga she'd got used to having

Liam around again. Used to watching him from the kitchen counter stool as he cooked them dinner, or waiting until he finished his second coffee of the day to start a conversation.

It was worse, in a way, than after Iceland. Then, it had all been about sex. Now she wasn't allowed to touch him, because of her own stupid rules, so she had more time to notice the smaller, everyday things about him.

None of them, however, made her want to touch him any less.

She still dreamt about kissing him, making love to him, every night. And when she'd met Selena the yoga instructor, in all her toned, tanned, centred beauty, she hadn't been able to stop the surge of jealousy that had powered through her.

These were all things she was going to have to get a handle on—either as a co-parent with Liam or because after this week she'd never see him again.

Suddenly, she was itching to know which it would be.

She'd promised him a week; she couldn't rush him now. But she hated her future feeling so uncertain.

Ever since Anthony had torn away the future she'd confidently believed was hers—one with a big white wedding with celebrity guests, and a life in relative comfort and pleasure, with love and affection from a husband she trusted over everything—she'd always refused to put her future in the hands of others. But now it seemed she had no choice. Until Liam made his decision, she couldn't plan anything at all.

And she was *itching* to plan.

Towelling herself off after her shower, she pulled on her comfiest shorts and T-shirt and dropped to sit on the bed.

There was no real way to tell the future, she knew that. But even a clue would help…

Rooting around in her rucksack, she pulled out the small silk bag that held her grandma's Tarot cards.

Maybe they couldn't give her the certainty she needed about what would happen next in her life, but perhaps they could help her get her swirling thoughts in order before Liam got home.

No, not home. Back to the treehouse. She *really* couldn't afford to start thinking of this place as home.

She grabbed herself a fruit tea from the kitchen, then added a water jug and glass from the fridge to the tray and took the whole lot out onto the balcony and placed it on the table. Then she took a seat, cross-legged in the wide wooden chair at the table, just across from the hammock where Liam had been sleeping since she'd arrived.

It only took a moment to lay out the cloth she used for her readings, but she spent a little longer shuffling the cards and thinking about her questions while she held them.

Her grandmother had always tried to teach her to read the cards properly, but Jenny hadn't been interested. Then, by the time she was, she was busy and working and there was never enough time to get into it when she visited.

And then her world had fallen apart, and Grandma had sent the cards to her without a note.

Grandma had died a few months later, before Jenny had even managed to ask her why.

Cards shuffled, she set out her favourite simple spread—three cards representing her past, present and future. Then she squinted at them and tried to figure out what they meant.

'What are you doing?'

She jumped at Liam's voice behind her, knocking the pack of cards so they fanned out across the table.

'You have *got* to stop sneaking up on me,' she said, one hand clutched to her chest. 'It's bad for the baby.' *And my heart.*

'Sorry.' He slid into the chair opposite her. 'But really. What are you doing?'

'Reading Tarot cards.' She used to be embarrassed when people found out about her little habit, but she'd grown to be confident in it. What did it matter to her what others thought of her anyway? 'They were my grandmother's.'

'And you believe they can tell the future?' She could hear the scepticism in his voice and, for a moment, wanted to play with him, to pretend that she did.

But honesty was going to be the most important thing between them going forward, and she didn't want to risk that, even for a joke.

'No, I don't,' she told him. 'But Grandma always used to do a reading for me when I visited, and somehow it always helped to get my thoughts in order. I still couldn't tell what was going to happen next, but I had a better handle on what I wanted, and what I'd do, if that makes any sense?'

Liam looked more intrigued than sceptical now. 'I think so. Can you show me?'

Jenny considered, watching him carefully for any sign that he was mocking her. She didn't find one.

It felt like a strangely personal thing to share—not because the cards had any spiritual meaning to her but because they'd come from her grandma. The only family member who hadn't completely abandoned her when her world had fallen apart.

But if Liam was going to be part of her life, even only as a friend and a co-parent, he deserved to know who she really was. And if she wanted his secrets she already knew she'd have to be willing to give up a few of her own.

Maybe the cards could help her do that, at least.

She nodded and said, 'Okay, then. I'll read one card for you. But I warn you, I'm not very good.'

Liam watched curiously as Jenny gathered up the scattered cards and patted them back into a pack between careful hands. She was such a practical, efficient sort of person, planning for the future rather than guessing at it, that he was surprised to discover this side to her.

He was also interested to hear about her grandmother. She'd not mentioned any other family and from the way she talked about her grandma, she wasn't around any longer. Did that mean she was all alone in the world now, apart from Winter? And the baby, of course.

And perhaps even him.

She handed the cards to him and straightened the silk cloth she'd covered the table with. She'd arrived with only a small suitcase and smaller backpack, so if she'd included these cards and their cloth in her minimalist packing they must be really important to her.

He felt as if he was finally seeing behind the curtain of Jenny Bouchard, and it was far more fascinating than any hokey attempts to tell his future.

'What do I do?' The cards felt worn and warm in his hands. *Well loved.* The thought came unbidden.

'Shuffle them,' she replied.

'Any particular way?' It felt disrespectful to fan the cards together as if he was playing poker with his buddies.

But Jenny shook her head. 'Whatever feels right to you.'

He shuffled the cards gingerly, somewhere between just cutting them and a half-hearted ripple. When he went to hand them back to Jenny, she shook her head.

'Put them down on the cloth,' she instructed, and he did so. 'Now, cut the pack wherever feels right.'

There was no particular feeling that led him to cutting it towards the bottom of the pack, but she seemed satisfied anyway.

'Now, take the top card and turn it over,' she said.

Liam did as he was told, and stared at a naked man and woman, with a snake climbing a tree beside her. The Lovers, the card read. Adam and Eve in the Garden of Eden, he realised. Temptation in all its forms.

He looked up at Jenny, who sighed. 'Of course.'

'I guess I can pretty much make up the interpretation of this one myself,' he joked.

She squinted at the card, and he knew she was deciding how much to tell him.

'Yes and no,' she said finally. 'The Lovers is a card about relationships, sure. But more than that, it's about choices, really. I mean, you pick one path—or one partner—and you say goodbye to your option on the rest. It's about decisions to be made about relationships, about the sacrifice that might involve, and about temptation, of course. Of the heart and the flesh, I suppose. And...' She trailed off.

'And?' he prompted.

'Grandma always used to say this card was about the loss of innocence too. Because of the Garden of Eden symbolism, I suppose. She said it reminded us that there was no coming back from a bad decision once it was made.'

'Hmm.' Liam sat back in his chair. When he'd thought it was about sex, and wanting but not touching, it had seemed the perfect card for them. Now she'd explained it more fully, it seemed agonisingly even more correct. If he chose to walk away at the end of this week, to sign away his parental rights to his child, that was it. There was no coming back from that decision. 'I guess I see what you mean about the cards showing you your present more than your future.'

'Right?' She gave him a lopsided, almost

ironic smile. 'It's because all they really are—
the cards, I mean—are stories in pictures.
They're symbols that remind us of tales we've
heard or things we've seen. And we interpret
them based on where we are in our lives.'

He frowned. 'How do you mean?'

'Well, if I hadn't shown up here this week
and you'd seen that card, you wouldn't have
been thinking about the decision you need
to make about the baby. You'd have been
thinking about… I don't know…whether it
was time to meet someone new, or stay alone
for ever.'

'Or whether to call that hot girl from Iceland next time I was in LA.'

She flashed him a grin at that, and he returned it for a moment before going back to
staring at the card.

'Except if you weren't here I wouldn't
be looking at a Tarot card at all. And now
I am…'

He shook his head, unsure how to finish
the sentence. But Jenny did it for him.

'We've only got a few days left.'

'Yeah.' Three more days and she'd be walking away—either for ever or ready for them
to start some complicated time-share parent-

ing agreement that neither of them knew how to do.

Why was she doing this? Suddenly he had to know. To understand why she was putting herself through this, this way.

'Why did you come here, really?' he asked.

She looked surprised at the question. 'You know why. Would you rather I hadn't? That I'd kept the baby a secret from you?'

Yes, a small part of his mind whispered. Because then he wouldn't have had to make decisions about a future he didn't trust.

But that wasn't the largest part of him. 'No,' he said, frustrated with himself for not being able to make sense of all this yet. 'I guess I just… You're young and beautiful and fun and clever and lovely. Why are you settling for a future of co-parenting with me, rather than out searching for your true love and happy ever after?' She worked for Winter. She had to know it was possible, that it could be out there for her somewhere. Why didn't she want it?

Jenny didn't answer, looking away as she tidied up the cards. There was a story here, one he'd sensed from the first moment he'd known about the baby. And he was damned if he wasn't going to get it out of her at last.

'Even in Iceland you were adamant that nothing between us could be anything more than a fling,' he remembered.

'So were you!' she shot back.

'Yeah, and I had good reasons.' He leant closer across the table until she looked up at him. 'I want to know what yours were.'

She held his gaze for a long moment, but he'd been doing this longer than her and she finally broke away.

'I had…a bad experience with love. I know what it can do and, honestly? Whatever the supposed wonders of true love, I'm not interested.'

'What happened?'

The pause that followed was long enough to make him wonder if she was busy coming up with a lie, but when she spoke the raw vulnerability and hesitation in her voice told him it was the truth.

'I was young. I got my first big break as an actress on a TV show, filming in Canada. I was starstruck.' She shrugged, and Liam felt a slightly sick feeling flowing through him as he filled in the blanks.

'You fell in love with a co-star.' It was too familiar a story. Working so closely together, away from the real world, it happened all the time—especially when people spent their days pretending to be in love with each other for the cameras. It was only a small step from that to making it happen in real life.

Sometimes it was the real thing, like Winter and Josh. Others...

She nodded. 'Anthony. He was married.'

Liam winced. 'It ended badly, I assume?'

'Of course it did.' She rippled the cards through her hands again, looking at them, not him. Liam suspected she hadn't needed the cards to tell her that would happen, but she'd put her faith in the power of love anyway.

She'd been young, she'd said. He thought she meant 'hopeful'.

'He told me his marriage was a sham,' she went on, not looking up. 'That it was all for the cameras anyway, and any love that had ever been between them had dried up years ago. He'd never cared about anything, anyone else enough to want to end it though...'

'Until he met you.' Disgust curled through him as he pictured it. Jenny, young and naive and enthusiastic, not even understanding the situation she was walking into.

He'd been in similar positions in his youth—older women who'd wanted to use him to make their husbands jealous, or for the shock value in the press. It had never been about him, just how he'd looked on their arm, or on camera.

It had stung, when he'd realised. But he'd never really fallen in love with any of them.

Jenny had.

'Yeah.' She placed the cards in a neat stack on the table and looked up at him at last. 'You can probably imagine what happened next. I thought we were going to ride off into the sunset together and live happily ever after and he—'

'Went back to his wife.'

'Yeah.' Her fingers twitched towards the cards, but she didn't pick them up again. 'And that should have been the end of it, right? Except he was famous. Not Winter and Josh or you famous, but he was famous enough. And so was she. So the papers got hold of it and for a month or more it was *everywhere*.'

Something clicked in Liam's brain. The first time he'd seen Jenny, on TV at a press conference Winter had given before she'd come to Iceland, he'd thought she looked familiar. But he hadn't been able to place where from, at the time.

Now, he knew. He'd seen her in countless grainy photos in newspapers and online, around six years ago. He hadn't paid them much attention then—it was just one more juicy scandal that the press got excited about for a month or two then forgot all about.

'What happened?' he asked, his voice steely. Whatever it was, he was sure he didn't want to hear it.

But he would, for her.

Whatever it was had scarred her, damaged her the way his accident had damaged him. He recognised that same weight of responsibility, of knowing that if either of them had made different choices, had lived their lives to a different code, they wouldn't be where they were now.

Losing Julie, and the baby, it had broken him for good. But maybe there was a way back for Jenny, a way he could help her find, even.

So when she paused he added, 'Tell me, Jenny.'

CHAPTER NINE

SHE DIDN'T WANT to tell him.

Having an affair with a married man—whatever lies he'd told her about his wife and the state of his marriage, however many times he'd promised he'd divorce his wife and marry her—remained the most shameful thing she'd ever done in her life.

But losing him, realising his lies, wasn't what had completely destroyed her belief in love. Obliterated her faith in people, and her ability to trust.

It was the next part that was the hardest to tell.

'When they saw it in the papers…my parents were horrified,' she said. 'My whole family, really. They'd always believed that going into acting would be my downfall and, right then, well, it seemed like they were right.'

It had been her dream, acting. When she'd

got her big break she'd honestly felt like all her hard work was paying off, her dreams were coming true.

But then it had emerged that she'd only been cast because the star—who had a phenomenal amount of sway on the show—had wanted to sleep with her, according to an anonymous source on set. Viewers started commenting on posts with the most vitriolic hate for her, her morals and, worst of all, her acting skills.

And her family…

'They believed everything that people were saying about me.' The words came out as a whisper. 'Every awful thing—every lie, and every truth, without ever trying to discern between the two.'

And a lot of it *had* been lies. The affair, such as it was, had been a small, low-key romance, compared to what she'd seen between celebrities since, while working for Winter. There hadn't been expensive presents or exotic trips away. She hadn't been flaunted on the red carpet or caught in seedy circumstances by the paparazzi.

There'd been flirting on set, and stolen moments together. Whispered promises and kisses that spoke of more. There'd been two afternoons in a nearby hotel, but never overnight. And that had been all.

Until he'd insisted on taking her out for dinner one night, and they'd been photographed kissing by a news photographer at another table, and that was it.

'The worst part was, I discovered later that he'd called that photographer himself, to make sure he was there to take the photo of us.' All along, she'd been nothing but a publicity ploy. She'd been in love. He'd been... Well. Using her was the nicest way she could finish that sentence.

Liam wasn't as polite, swearing under his breath as he took in the implications of her words.

'Anyway. I got fired from the show, of course—at his behest, I imagine.' It still hurt—a deep-down ache that would never go away, she suspected—that someone had taken her dream away from her so easily, without any thought for her at all. Worse still was the feeling that she might not have deserved it in the first place.

'And your family?' Liam's question was low, urgent, and she knew he'd homed in on the part of this story that pained her most of all, even after so long.

'They disowned me.' It wasn't the whole story—that involved lots of tense conversations with her mother, her father leaving the room whenever she entered it, and the heartbreaking realisation that her family were happier when she wasn't around, even after the newspapers had moved on and there wasn't a man with a camera camped in the bushes outside their house every morning. But it was how it felt, and where it ended. 'All except my grandmother, but she lived with my parents and didn't get much say on what went on in the house. And she died just a few months later, anyway.'

'And you were alone.' There was something else in his voice this time. Not just pity, or even anger on her behalf. An understanding she hadn't expected to find from him.

Except he'd been left alone too, hadn't he? After the accident. She might not know the details, but she knew that much from things Winter and Josh had said.

He'd been alone ever since.

'I wasn't alone for long, though,' she said. She didn't want him feeling sorry for her, even if this was something they could bond over. 'I moved to LA, started over. And instead of endless rounds of auditions where people looked at me like they sort of recognised me, then smirked when they figured out where from, I got the job working for Winter instead. And it was the best thing that could have ever happened to me.'

'You don't miss acting?'

It was a question she'd asked herself, often, over the past five years. Her dream job had been taken away from her, and she hated the idea that she'd given up on it since then. But... when she looked back at her time working as an actress, she knew that the biggest appeal had been her on-set romance. She'd always felt as if she'd just been told what to do, shuffled around and fed lines to say. And maybe that was different for other actors—she knew that Josh and Winter loved becoming other people on film. But for her it didn't feel that way.

She hadn't been surprised when Winter had decided to try directing either. The idea of having control over something sounded far more appealing than just doing what she was told.

And working for Winter… If her boss had been anybody else, then maybe being a personal assistant would have felt much the same as acting had—as if she was being told what to do all the time. But it wasn't like that with Winter.

Winter trusted her. She gave her space and autonomy and responsibility. Once Jenny had proven she was up to the job, Winter let her do it however she saw fit. She was in charge of their itineraries, organising travel and accommodation, gatekeeping people who wanted access to Winter's time. But she was also a respected advisor; Winter talked to her about projects before deciding whether to take them on, and she listened to her thoughts and opinions too. They were a team, even now she was back together with Josh, and Jenny found she enjoyed that far more than she'd ever liked acting.

'I really don't,' she answered finally. 'I thought I would but… I've found something else. Something that suits me far better. I like working for Winter—no, I love it. I'm good at it, I'm well paid for it and I enjoy it. Why would I want to do anything else?'

He gave her a wry smile. 'You're lucky

to have figured that out—to find what you love and make it a career. Too many people never do.'

Was he talking about himself? Jenny remembered how fast he'd shut her down when she'd asked him about acting in the car yesterday. But now she'd spilled all her secrets... maybe he'd be ready to share some of his?

Or not. Liam Delaney didn't seem like the sort to share easily.

She took a deep breath and asked anyway.

He knew the question was coming from the look on her face—as if she was steeling herself against a knockback.

'What about you? You said there was nothing left for you in acting. But do you miss it, all the same?'

Did he *miss* it? He could barely even remember it.

Liam looked away, staring out over the balcony into the rainforest, letting the sounds of nature around him fill the silence.

He didn't want to answer her question, but he knew he owed her some reciprocal sharing. She'd spilled her secrets, helped him understand why she wasn't searching for a happily

ever after to go with the baby he'd accidentally gifted her. And he *did* understand. Trust,
once lost, was the hardest thing to regain.

She'd lost faith in love, in family, in people
in general—of course she wasn't going to be
looking to take another chance on love.

But he'd lost faith in himself. And he didn't
know how to explain that to her.

'I don't *miss* it, exactly,' he said, searching
for the right words. 'It's more like it was a
part of my life I barely recognise any longer.'
He sure as hell didn't recognise the person
he'd been back then—and he didn't want to.

'So you really won't ever go back to it?'

The wistfulness in her question surprised
him. 'Why? You a fan?'

'Isn't everybody?' She raised her eyebrows
at him across the table. 'You were kind of a
star.'

'And that was the problem.' He didn't want
to tell her. But he owed her some sort of ex-
planation for his lifestyle choices—as the
mother of his child, if nothing else. He sighed
and groped for the right words. 'I liked being
a star far more than I enjoyed acting. I liked
the attention, the parties. The drink and the
drugs. The chance to live the wild, uninhib-

ited life I thought I was entitled to.' God, how he hated to think of the man he'd been back then.

Jenny stayed silent, waiting for him to continue, which he appreciated. Getting this out was hard enough. Dealing with questions about it would be impossible.

'I was an idiot. Worse. I was all those bad words you can't say on screen if you want a family-friendly rating. And I couldn't even see it.' He reached for the jug of water with slices of citrus fruits in that sat at the centre of the table and poured himself a glass. 'Other people tried to tell me—Josh, especially. But I couldn't hear them over my own ego. I was living the kind of life I thought film stars were *supposed* to live. And then I met Julie.'

She'd been an actress too, of course. He was a film star; who else was he supposed to date? She'd been blonde and beautiful and waif-thin for the cameras—and she'd liked to party as much as he had. He'd thought he'd loved her, believed it through the fog of alcohol and partying, but some days he wondered whether they'd just fallen down into the same hole together and that was the only thing that kept them as a couple.

'I remember seeing photos of the two of you together,' Jenny said softly. 'You were a beautiful couple.'

There was something behind her words, an emotion it took him a moment to get hold of. When he realised what it was, he almost laughed.

Not jealousy, he thought. Pity. Which he could understand, but he really didn't deserve.

Liam had made a practice, over the last five years, of being brutally honest with himself at all times. It was the only way he'd found to keep himself on a path that didn't lead to self-destruction. The moment he let himself believe that one drink, one party, one slip-up wouldn't ruin him, he'd be done for. He knew that about himself.

He was an absolutist—an all-or-nothing kind of person. It was just better for everyone around him if he stuck with nothing.

But brutal honesty had saved him. And the more time he spent with Jenny, thinking about a future he'd been avoiding for half a decade, the more he realised that brutal honesty was the only thing that was going to get them through this too.

'I loved Julie,' he said bluntly. 'But if you're thinking the reason I won't open myself up to a relationship again is because I'm still in love with a ghost, you're wrong. I'm not the same man who loved Julie, and if she hadn't died it wouldn't have lasted between us.'

'Why not?'

'Because I'd have screwed it up. Because I *was* a screw-up, and I only got my head on straight because of the accident.' How long could he have continued down the path of self-destruction he'd been on, otherwise? He shuddered to think. And he knew it would never have ended well, for anybody.

'When you left Hollywood.'

'Yeah.' He had to tell her the rest of it, he knew that. But how?

'And you're a success now,' Jenny went on, not looking up at him. 'You turned your life around, you straightened yourself out, and you build these incredible retreat hotels for people who need to escape from the real world for a while, because that's what you needed after the accident, right?'

'Yeah,' Liam said again. 'That's right.'

She lifted her chin and met his gaze. 'You've done all that, Liam. But what's next?

I mean, you say you're not still hung-up on your dead ex-girlfriend, but you're not moving on either, are you? And trust me, I understand not wanting to risk falling in love again. But we have the chance of a different sort of future now, and I guess I'm wondering what's holding you back from taking it.'

It was a fair question—one that anyone else would have asked long before now. But Jenny had given him the space he needed to work through his initial emotions about her announcement. And their week was running out.

He needed to face up to exactly what was standing in the way of his future—any future. And Jenny had a right to know what it was.

'Julie was pregnant when she died.' Rip the sticking plaster off, get the horrors out of his head and onto the table between them. Jenny's gasp barely penetrated his fog of memories. 'Ten weeks. We were over the moon, in the naïve way you are when everything still feels like an adventure. That's why she was driving—I was off my head, celebrating the news, even though we'd known for a few weeks, and she was the sober one for a change, trying to do the right thing for the baby.'

She'd wanted to go home, he remembered. She'd been tired, a little nauseous, and grumpy as all hell because she couldn't drink and he could. She'd wanted to go home and he'd asked her to stay. Told her she was no fun, that being parents didn't have to change them. That they still deserved to live their lives, not mortgage their happiness to the kid. That if that was what she wanted him to do, she should leave now.

She hadn't left. She'd stayed, and waited to drive his drunk arse home from the party. But she'd been tired—exhausted. And she'd missed a red light he'd been too drunk to even see, and the other car had come from seemingly nowhere.

And in a moment that dream of a perfect, easy life had disappeared.

'I'm… God, Liam. I'm so sorry.' Reaching across the table, she grabbed his hand and squeezed. 'I had no idea.'

'Her family managed to keep it out of the papers, thank God. I was in no state to do it. I was in no state to do much of anything, really.' Even his memories of that time were hazy, which he could only assume was for the best. 'Eventually, I dragged myself to some rehab centre in the middle of the desert and… Well. Sorted myself out. Learned some coping strategies and so on. But I knew I could never go back to the life I'd had before—and I didn't even want to.'

'I'm not surprised,' Jenny murmured. 'I know a little about how that feels.'

She did, Liam realised as he thought back over their stories. Their experiences had been very different, of course, but the bones of them… They'd both made mistakes and paid for them. They'd both lost, and they'd both found a way to keep on living. To put the past behind them and find a new present to exist in.

But now the future had come calling. For both of them.

'I think you do. And I hope that means you'll understand when I say this.' Liam turned his hand over under her palm, clasping her fingers in his own. 'If I could fall in love again then this, with you and the baby, could be a second chance for me—some sort of redemption, even. But I can't. Love is not in my cards, because I know—the same way you do—how it leads to loss and pain, and I know I couldn't survive that twice. It almost killed me last time and…to my shame, I'm not strong enough to risk that again. So if we do this, if we decide to co-parent this child, that is all we can ever be. Friends, perhaps, if we're lucky. But I need you to know I'll never be able to give you anything more.'

If he'd seen doubt in her face, if he'd thought for a moment she was hoping for more—chasing a fairy tale ending he couldn't provide—he'd have walked away right then and there.

But instead he saw reflected back in her eyes the very same emotions that filled his own heart.

Resignation, tinged with sadness perhaps, but solid and firm all the same. Liam felt his shoulders drop as he relaxed.

They were two broken people making their way in a world that wanted them to be whole again but couldn't tell them how to get there.

This chance at a future was the best either of them was likely to get, he realised as the last of his reservations about the situation began to crumble.

Maybe this *was* his second chance, after all.

CHAPTER TEN

'WE'RE NOT TAKING the four-by-four today?'
Jenny asked, confused, as Liam handed the
car keys to one of his employees.

'Not today.' Liam turned to pick up a small
backpack stocked, Jenny knew, with water,
bug-repellent, sunscreen and snacks. 'Today,
we're doing something different. There are
no roads where I want to take you, so today,
we're exploring on foot.'

Their mode of transport wasn't the only
thing about today that was different, Jenny
reflected as she shouldered her own backpack and followed him out of the main clearing where the temporary office for his new
retreat was based, and down an almost hidden path through the thickening rainforest.

After their soul-baring conversation the
night before, the air between them felt lighter,
in lots of ways. They'd put their secrets out

there and found they had more in common than they'd imagined. Liam wasn't avoiding relationships and love because of a permanently broken heart, but for the same reasons she was.

Because love couldn't be trusted to stay. One way or another, love broke everyone—whether it was now or in fifty years, if you were one of the lucky ones.

Liam and Jenny already knew they weren't the lucky ones.

But at least they were on the same page. Love wasn't going to be a factor in whatever followed next and, with their secrets shared, neither of them had to worry any longer that the other would be expecting more than they could give. That helped Jenny relax about the situation.

Of course she was still pregnant by an ex-movie star she wasn't in a relationship with, and now she knew about his ex-girlfriend's pregnancy...well, it made it a lot easier to understand why Liam might be pulling back from the situation.

Still, she had a good feeling about things as they headed off into the rainforest for the short hike Liam had promised would astound and amaze her. After quite a few days in the rainforest, and after visiting—if not experiencing—the hot springs and the beach and staying in the most incredible treehouse she could imagine, she was intrigued to find out what else there was to see that could be *more* amazing.

Around her, the rainforest canopy closed overhead, darkening their path. She couldn't see another soul ahead on the trail, or behind them, but she knew the greenery that surrounded them was teeming with life. With every step, she heard the buzz and hum of insects; birds called out overhead and the trees rustled with the movement of hidden creatures.

Liam came to a sudden stop in front of her—so sudden that, as he turned towards her, she found herself pressed up against his glistening skin.

'Look,' he breathed under his breath, indicating towards the trees with the smallest motion, obviously trying to avoid drawing the attention of whatever he'd spotted.

Hyperaware that his body was closer to hers than it had been since the day she'd arrived, Jenny tried to concentrate on what he was showing her. She sucked in a breath as she spotted it.

There, sprawled out over the branch of a tree just above their heads off the path, was a furry black body with oversized hands and feet, a black tail curled around the branch behind him.

'A howler monkey,' Liam breathed. 'You've probably heard them in the mornings, but we're lucky to spot one here.'

'Is it sleeping?' It looked like it had settled in for a siesta, the way Jenny wanted to most afternoons since she'd got pregnant.

'Probably. They sleep a lot. And when they're not sleeping—'

He broke off as the monkey shifted. Jenny held her breath as they waited to see if he'd wake up…

In one swift movement, the howler monkey leapt up onto the branch on all fours, raised his head and howled.

Jenny couldn't help but laugh with delight, and beside her Liam did the same—even as the monkey scampered off through the trees, leaping from branch to branch.

'I wonder what else we'll see,' Liam said as they set off again.

The trail was only wide enough for one of them to pass at a time and, since Liam was the one who ostensibly knew where he was going, it made sense for Jenny to follow behind.

If she also appreciated the fact that it meant she got to admire his ass in his shorts, or the width of his shoulders under his backpack, well, she was keeping that to herself.

Because there was another fact last night had brought to life—one she couldn't quite shake, even if it receded slightly as they stopped to admire a sloth lolling under a tree branch, or macaws and toucans flying overhead.

They were getting closer to making a decision about whether they were going to parent this child together. Soon, she'd be leaving Costa Rica—and perhaps Liam—behind.

And they'd only sworn to keep their hands off each other until they made a firm decision about the future.

She'd worked so hard to put thoughts of Liam and her together out of her head, but it wasn't exactly easy. Their entire relationship before she'd come to Costa Rica was based only on sex. Learning more about who he was as a man—the lengths he'd gone to in order to overcome his past flaws, for instance—didn't exactly make her want him any less.

The heat she felt every time his gaze caught hers or his hand brushed against her side, or even if he *smiled* at her, wasn't helping either. And she had a sneaking suspicion he felt the same.

They'd agreed no sex until they'd made a decision. And they'd agreed they'd make a decision before she left Costa Rica at the end of the week.

They *hadn't* said they couldn't make the decision sooner and enjoy whatever time they had left together any way they pleased...

'Ah, here we go,' Liam said up ahead, and Jenny shook away her inappropriate thoughts to focus on whatever wonder of the natural world he'd found to show her this time.

Except this time it wasn't the natural world at all.

'Oh!' The path opened up into a clearing not unlike the one they'd started in, except this one was finished. There were no luxury treehouses as such, but there were a few cabins on stilts, and Jenny could see that they grew in numbers as the site got closer to the beach, just visible through the rainforest.

'Is that the beach we visited the other day?' She didn't remember seeing any cabins, but then she'd been a little distracted that day.

Liam shook his head. 'The next one along.'

'I didn't realise how far we'd walked.' Too busy staring at his ass.

He gave her a smirk and a warm look, as if he knew exactly what she was thinking. 'This resort is…not my competition, because we're after a different market of traveller. This place is for families, for a start, whereas mine is geared up for couples or solo travellers. But I thought you'd like to get a look at what it might look like when it's finished.'

Jenny turned slowly round to take in the sights. The main entrance to the resort was via a slightly garish arch on the road that ran parallel to the beach and led into this clearing where the main office sat. On a whim, she crossed to an oversized poster board next to it, filled with information about local attractions. Pictures of local wildlife bordered information about snorkelling lessons, diving trips and even a giant zip wire through the rainforest.

Her eyes widened at that. Heights weren't always her favourite, but she did love the rush of a zip wire—and moving through the rainforest from above, like the macaws and other birds did, had to be even more spectacular than sitting on the treehouse balcony.

A hand looped loosely around her wrist and Liam turned her away from the board. 'Whatever you're thinking, no. We're not done with our hike yet.' His gaze flicked towards the board for a moment and she thought she felt his grip tighten just slightly, not enough to hurt, before releasing again. 'And none of those things looks remotely safe for the baby.'

The diving trips probably had restrictions, and she could understand why the fast-moving beach buggies you could hire might make him nervous. But… 'Not even the zip wire?'

She wasn't imagining it; he definitely shuddered at that idea. 'Definitely not the zip wire. Come on. We'll get a drink and something to eat at the café here, then continue our hike.'

Jenny followed him as he moved towards another cabin on stilts, set out with pretty tables out front, but her mind stayed on his reaction to the activities board.

Safe for the baby.

For someone who was holding back, who three days ago hadn't known she couldn't drink too much coffee or go in the hot springs…she had a feeling that Liam was coming around. Had made a decision, even, about what happened next. And that gave her an extra bounce in her step as she followed him.

Because if he'd decided…well, then their self-imposed restrictions could come to an end.

And she couldn't quite stop herself smiling at that idea.

He shouldn't have made her walk in front of him.

The logic had been sound in his head. After they'd finished at the café, the trail he wanted to follow only went one way, so there was no need for him to lead the way to avoid getting lost. And he didn't want her first view of their destination to be blocked by his body—he wanted her to get the full impact the moment they arrived.

But that meant he was spending the whole hike staring at her legs in those shorts, and at the shorts themselves and the curvaceous rear end that they only just covered.

He forced his eyes higher, but even that just led him to her long blonde ponytail, fixed high on her head and bobbing with every step. Memories flooded his brain—memories of running his fingers through that hair, of seeing it splayed out on his pillow under her, or hanging down around her face as she rode him…

Liam blinked, swallowed, and forced himself to scan the trees for more howler monkeys. He needed the distraction.

While the question of what to do next hung between them it had been…well, not easy, but at least *possible* to keep Jenny at arm's length. But after last night's conversation Liam knew what he needed to do, even if he hadn't shared his decision with her just yet.

He wanted to give himself time to sit with his choice, make sure he was certain, before he did that. And even once he told her, there'd still be lots to sort out—money, for starters, and conversations about that always seemed to drag on, in his experience.

Deciding wasn't the end of anything.

Except the deal that they'd made, to keep their hands off each other until they had made up their minds on what happened next.

How far would she take that? he wondered idly, as the path beneath his feet twisted through the lush green vegetation. The air around them felt damp and humid, and he knew his shirt was sticking to his back under his rucksack.

Would she want all the 'i's dotted and the 't's crossed before she'd allow any closeness between them again? Or if he made the wrong choice—or even the right one—would she call time on anything physical between them anyway?

It was the not knowing that was driving him out of his mind. Not knowing if he'd ever get to touch her that way again. To kiss her. To hold her. To watch her fall apart in his arms from all the pleasure he could give her…

Up ahead, Jenny gasped as she turned the last bend—loud enough to send a bird fleeing from the nearest tree.

Liam smiled. They were there.

'Oh, my…that's the most beautiful thing I've ever seen!'

Liam scooted alongside her, as close as he could get, given the narrowness of the trail, and took in the awe and wonder on her face.

Then he turned to look at the mighty waterfall he'd brought her to see. From a cliff face high above, water cascaded down over the rocks, crashing over outcrops and sending up foam as it hit the river at the bottom. Even from a distance, the roar of the water filled the air.

Around it, the verdant rainforest seemed to blossom even more generously, with brightly coloured blooms and the ever-present sound of life, thriving in the trees and foliage. The canopy opened up enough to show an oval of bright blue sky overhead, letting in rays of sunlight that caught the water droplets at all angles, sending rainbows scattering around them.

Jenny was right; it was beautiful.

Just not as beautiful as her face as she gazed at it.

She turned at last and beamed up at him. 'Thank you for bringing me here.'

'I wanted you to see it,' he admitted, around the lump in his throat. 'Before you leave.'

The reference to her impending departure didn't even seem to register with her. 'Can we get closer?'

Closer meant the slippery wet rocks at the bottom of the waterfall—or worse, standing in the current itself. Liam had been here plenty of times before, and seen many other tourists enjoying the site, but this was different. This was Jenny, who was carrying his child, and suddenly all he could see was the dangers inherent in the place he'd brought her to.

And he'd thought talking her out of the zip wire was the worst of it.

She bounced on the balls of her feet like a child, and Liam gave in. 'Come on, then. But be careful on the rocks.' He took her hand and together they picked their way through the undergrowth, until they reached the waterfall itself.

His heart remained in his mouth the whole time she scampered around the flat rocks that covered the base of the falls, and he stayed on high alert, ready to catch her at the first sign of her feet slipping. But Jenny was surefooted and stayed firmly upright. Still, he was relieved when at last she stepped back onto dry land, with him right behind her.

The sun overhead was starting to sink down behind the high trees surrounding them, a glorious golden glow still filling the clearing around the waterfall. They'd been lucky to have it to themselves for the afternoon, but he suspected some sunset-seekers might join them soon enough, and he wanted them both safely back in his treehouse before the rainforest grew too dark. He had torches in his bag, but he'd rather not need to use them.

'Ready to head back?'

'Hmm?' Jenny remained staring at the waterfall, and in the moment Liam couldn't help but give in to just a little of the romanticism of it all. Or maybe just the temptation that was Jenny Bouchard herself.

He stepped up behind her, his arms wrapping easily around her waist as her backpack lay on the grass by her feet. She tensed for only a second before relaxing into his embrace, resting her head against his chest.

And just for a moment Liam had the strangest sensation of everything in the world being right.

Then she turned in his arms, looked up at him, and he saw the familiar heat in her eyes, and knew that everything could be a hell of a lot better if they just made a choice and gave up that stupid no sex rule.

'Liam…' Her tongue darted out to swipe over her lips, and he felt his blood warm and his body harden in response. Damn it, if such a tiny movement could affect him this way, if she actually kissed him he might have to take her on the spot. Which could possibly traumatise any approaching tourists for life, and maybe get them arrested.

'We should get back,' he said, his voice betraying him and coming out low and raspy. 'To the treehouse, I mean. Before it gets dark.'

'I know. I just…' She broke off, and he saw the helplessness in her eyes.

At least it wasn't just him. If the physical connection between them hadn't affected her the same way, he wasn't sure how he'd have lived with it.

It wouldn't last for ever, he was sure. A child—that was a for ever commitment, and one he'd made without even intending to. But he could keep that separate from this…thing with Jenny, couldn't he?

Because, whatever happened between them in the future, he knew he had to have her again.

CHAPTER ELEVEN

THEY WERE STANDING close enough that Jenny could feel the heat of his breath, the warmth of his skin—and if she pressed in just a little closer she'd know for sure whether their proximity was affecting him as much as it was her.

She wanted to. She wanted, needed, to feel him hard against her again.

But first they had decisions to make. And probably the middle of a popular tourist destination in a rainforest wasn't the place to do that.

Or was it? They hadn't seen anyone else all day. Maybe the only people who'd see them were the howler monkeys…

Focus, Jenny.

Decisions. She needed to know what Liam had decided before they could go any further. That was the key obstacle to just seducing him here in the middle of the rainforest.

They could figure out the details later, but he had to decide if he was in or out. Until she knew that…her whole future was still in flux. And she wasn't going to make that worse by giving in to their mutual lust.

A small part of her brain whispered that once he'd got what he wanted from her, what reason would he have to make a firm decision at all? She couldn't risk it.

'I want to kiss you so much right now.' Liam's hand clenched against her hip, and a muscle in his jaw twitched with the apparent restraint he was forcing on himself.

God, she loved that. Loved that this man— who'd spent years turning himself from an impulsive, careless star into a controlled businessman—wanted her so much his whole body was rebelling.

She couldn't resist. Not completely. She pressed a little closer and felt that familiar hard ridge behind his shorts, and knew he was every bit as out of control as she was when it came to the chemistry between them.

But chemistry wasn't love, or trust. It wasn't certainty or safety.

Even if it was a hell of a lot of fun.

Liam's eyes fluttered closed and, with her

brain fighting her body, Jenny stepped away. Not far, just enough that they weren't actually touching any more.

Touching seemed unfair, given what she was about to say next.

'We promised each other we wouldn't let our libidos interfere with the decision we had to make.' And he understood now why that mattered so much to her, she hoped. Now he knew the kind of trouble her heart and her body—not to mention an overdeveloped sense of romance—had got her into before.

It was a point of pride to Jenny that she never made the same mistake twice.

'Then I think we need to make a decision pretty damn quick, don't you?' Liam's voice was strained. 'Because, honestly, I think my libido is tired of waiting on my brain.'

She couldn't help but laugh at that, and the small smile he gave her told her that her amusement had been his aim all along. But he also had a good point.

'Are you ready to do that? To make a decision about being a father or not?' In an instant, all laughter disappeared between them.

Because this was important. It wasn't just their future—or the possibility of slaking

the need for another night together. This was
about their *child's* future, and Jenny trusted
him to take that every bit as seriously as she
did.

Even that amazed her, now she thought
about it. She trusted him to do this right—
even if that meant walking away. Other than
Winter, she couldn't think of another person
in the world she trusted as much these days.

'I think I am, yeah,' he said softly. 'No, not
think. I know. I'm ready.'

There was a steely certainty behind his
words, reassuring her that this wasn't a man
just saying whatever she needed to hear to
get her into bed. In fact, she knew there was
a good chance she *wasn't* going to like whatever he had to say at all.

But she'd respect it. She'd try to understand
it. Because she understood *him* a lot better
now—and the enormity of what she was asking him to do.

Liam Delaney had lost everything and
blamed himself for it. He'd pieced himself
back together from a darker place than she'd
ever been, and held himself there through
sheer force of will, and a distance from any-

thing that could lead him down that dark path again.

She was under no illusion that she wasn't asking him to risk it again, for their child.

Only he knew if he was ready for that, and she'd have to respect whatever conclusion he came to.

Some people aren't ready, or cut out to be parents, she reminded herself, thinking briefly of her own family.

She'd rather her baby have one loving parent than two parents whose love was conditional on them never making mistakes, or only being the person they thought they should be.

She'd rather he never be involved at all than walk away when their kid needed him. When they loved and trusted him.

She knew how that destroyed a person. Made them feel like they'd never been worth that love in the first place.

Nobody was going to do that to her baby.

'So—' she started, then cut herself off as the sound of voices reached them from the trail they'd arrived by.

Apparently, their peace and solitude in this magical place was over. She took another step back, out of his personal space, and reached for her backpack as a cover for the disappointment she felt.

'Let's have this conversation back at the treehouse.' Liam's voice was still low and husky, and she felt it humming through her body. 'I think we're going to want some privacy for it. And after it.'

The promise in his words seemed to thicken her blood, until she could feel it pulsing through all her most sensitive parts.

After.

As much as she wanted to hear his decision, she had to admit that *after* was never going to be far from her mind… She needed to make sure she didn't let it take over. Her brain had to stay in charge here, not her body. A little distance and time from feeling him pressed up against her might help with that.

Time, distance and possibly a cold shower.

She hoisted her backpack up onto her shoulders again. 'Then let's get moving.'

The hike back to the treehouse helped Liam gain control of his body and mind at least a little before they talked—helped by the fact he insisted on leading the way, so he wasn't staring at Jenny's long, toned legs all the way home. But even as he shut the door behind them, and Jenny announced she needed a shower before they talked, he could still feel the tension.

They were going to sort this, one way or another, tonight.

With that in mind, he prepared by calling out for food, pouring them both a non-alcoholic drink and making sure the living space looked as cosy and friendly as it was possible for a luxury treehouse in a rainforest to look, before taking his own turn in the shower.

As the cool water battered against his sweat-salted skin, he ran over his decision in his mind one last time, determined to ensure he was making the right one.

Then he switched off the water and let the sudden silence lull him into calm as he towelled off and dressed, ready to face Jenny again.

'Food's here,' she said softly as he padded back into the living area. Dressed in a soft, loose T-shirt over shorts that clung to her every curve, she sat cross-legged on the sofa, a plate of the same local food they'd eaten the first night balanced on her lap. Her damp hair was piled up on the top of her head, with just a few tendrils clinging to her neck and hanging against her cheeks. Skin scrubbed clean, her face glowed a healthy pink, but her eyes were wary.

What had *she* been thinking about in the shower? What was she expecting from him now? And was he about to live up—or down—to expectations?

Behind it all, the heat between them still lingered. He felt it in her gaze as she watched him fix his own plate and take a seat in the armchair opposite her. It wouldn't do to be too close for this conversation, he knew.

They ate in silence for long minutes, neither risking looking at the other too long. But, as much as he'd ordered to replenish them after their hike, he couldn't draw the meal out for ever.

'So.' Jenny swallowed her last mouthful of food and looked up at him. 'You've made a decision?'

He nodded. 'Yeah. I have.' He forked some extra rice and beans onto his plate, then into his mouth, to buy him a little time before saying anything more. He had to get this right, and that meant not jumping in with both feet the way he always did. No, the way he *used* to.

He wasn't that man any more. And that was the only reason he could make this decision at all.

'Care to share?' From the look on her face, Jenny was wise to his tactics.

He didn't rush, though.

'You know now, I think, how much of a shock your news was to me. And why my first reaction was, quite honestly, terror,' he said.

'Because of Julie. And the baby you lost.' Her words were quiet, gentle, but she wasn't shying away from what he'd told her or couching his tragedy in careful euphemisms. Good. They needed to be clear and honest about this. It was the only way it was going to work.

'I'm still scared,' he admitted. 'I'd made the decision that a family wasn't in the cards for me, and you coming here has turned the life I was living, the life I expected to have, upside down.'

'It wasn't exactly planned on my part either, you realise.' There was a touch of annoyance in her voice.

'I know. I wasn't…' He took a breath and started again. 'What I'm trying to say is, it took me a little time to get accustomed to the idea. The thought of being a father.' He'd never be the kind of father his own had been, Liam knew. But he also knew he had to try.

'And now you've got used to it? What are you going to do?'

That was the only question that mattered, wasn't it?

'I want to be a part of the baby's life. I want to try…to be a good father.' He scanned her face for a reaction, but she kept her expression completely neutral—perhaps sensing that he wasn't finished yet. 'But I can't offer you any more. I can't give you love or for ever. I'm not going to marry you just because I got you pregnant—' He held up a hand when she started to interject. 'And I know you wouldn't want that anyway.'

'Damn straight,' she muttered. 'I *never* asked for that from you. I never would.'

'I know,' Liam replied. That wasn't the sort of woman she was. It was one of the things he liked most about her. And one of the reasons why he felt reasonably confident about the next part of his decision. 'But I *do* want us to be friends. Not just co-parents handing the baby over at the door without speaking.

I know that before this week we never really explored anything outside of the physical connection between us. But over the last few days… I like to think we've become friends.'

She gave him a small smile. 'So do I.'

'And I'd like to keep that,' he went on. 'I want us to parent our child together as friends and work together to give him or her the future they deserve.'

The smile grew. 'I can live with that.'

'Good.' For a long moment he held her gaze, basking in the warmth of that smile, and everything felt possible.

For a moment.

Then she jerked her head away, looking down at her hands. 'But what about…' She took a deep breath, then forced the words out. 'What happened at the waterfall…that's going to keep happening between us, isn't it? I mean, if we're around each other a lot…what do we do about the chemistry between us?'

It was a fair question, Liam knew—and one he'd given a lot of thought to over the past twenty-four hours. He wasn't sure how long his proposed answer would hold, but it was the only one he had for now.

'It seems to me that the physical connection we have…it's too strong to just ignore it. And it's so damn good that trying would seem a waste. Don't you think?'

A flash of heat in her eyes told him she agreed. 'So what do you suggest?'

Liam stood and moved around the table to sit beside her on the sofa. 'I think that, as long as we've got our ground rules straight, there's nothing wrong with being friends— and co-parents—with benefits, for as long as this chemistry lasts. Is there?'

Jenny stared at him as he sat beside her, the corner of his lips turned up in a one-sided half-smile, the same heat she'd seen by the waterfall still smouldering behind his eyes. Looking away, she reached for her water glass and tried to think.

She could say no, and she knew he'd accept it and walk away. He wouldn't push her or ask for any more than she was willing to give.

And he'd been very clear about what *he* could give.

Not love. Not for ever. Not the clichéd Hollywood happy-ever-after.

But that wasn't what she'd asked for anyway.

And what he could give…

Friendship. Respect. Someone to take on this crazy parenting journey with, so she wouldn't be alone in it.

Co-parents, that made sense. The relief that had trickled through her as his words sank in was proof that, even if she hadn't known it, even if she'd told herself over and over that she was happy doing this alone, his answer was the one she'd been hoping for all along.

And friends, she liked that too. Far better to be a team, and one working happily alongside each other. She *liked* Liam—not just his body, or the way he made her feel in bed. She liked him as a person, and that had been… not exactly a surprise, because she wasn't in the habit of falling into bed with people she didn't like. But the extent to which she enjoyed his company, felt comfortable talking to him, sharing things with him, she hadn't expected that when she'd arrived.

So. Friends who co-parented. That she was on board with.

But the benefits part…

For as long as this chemistry lasts.

That was the key part of his offer, wasn't it? He wasn't *expecting* it to last—and neither was she, really. Which meant she would have to guard her heart against believing it was anything more than lust between them. And she had to prepare for the day it was over too.

The end of their physical relationship would be another certainty to build into her model of the future—and she'd have to hope it would be mutual and amicable when it came.

Could she do that? Live waiting for that other shoe to drop?

And could she trust her heart not to fall too far, too fast, beyond what she knew he could give?

She studied his face again as he waited for her answer, never rushing her, or pushing. Just giving her the time and space to make her decision. He'd even shifted a little on the sofa to make sure there was clear space between them—not that it made any difference. She could remember the feel of his body against hers even if there was an ocean between them.

The heat they shared wasn't going away in a hurry, so they'd have to deal with it as coparents anyway. And yes, any purely physical arrangement wouldn't last between them, for logistical reasons or whatever, and she'd have to prepare for that. It was an added complication, for sure.

But the idea of never having Liam again… she couldn't bear that.

Really, he was offering her the best of all possible worlds here, wasn't he? A baby, a supportive friend to raise it with, her independence and freedom to shape her own future *and* great sex. Who could ask for anything more?

But she was going to be a mother. Which meant putting her child first.

'If our physical relationship ever interferes with our ability to parent our child together—'

'We end it,' Liam interrupted. 'In a heartbeat.'

His quick certainty reassured her. 'Agreed.'

And in that case what was there, really, holding her back?

She took a last sip of water, placed her glass on the table and turned to fall into his kiss.

CHAPTER TWELVE

TWO DAYS LATER Liam's body still hummed with pleasure as he stepped out of the shower and saw Jenny still dozing in the bed they'd barely left since they'd agreed on their new arrangement. God, he was tempted to climb back in and claim some more.

Except he had to, at some point, check in on the resort. He'd left everything he could in the hands of his employees this week—even more so over the last forty-eight hours—but he was the boss, and the buck stopped with him. So he'd go down to work.

And then he'd get back up here as fast as possible to slip between those sheets with Jenny again.

Pulling on shorts and a T-shirt, he bent down to place a kiss on Jenny's cheek, but she stirred and met his lips with her own instead.

'You're going?' Her voice was fuzzy with

sleep, her golden hair spread across his pillow, and it made him wonder if the guys couldn't manage on their own for just one more day…

'I just need to check in.' He brushed a lock of hair away from her eyes. 'I'll be back.'

'You're sure you have to go?' Her hands, warm from the covers, slid up his thighs as she kissed him again, and he felt his resistance melting away.

He shifted on the edge of the bed until he was practically lying over her, as Jenny's hands disappeared under his T-shirt, caressing the skin of his back, her nails scratching lightly across his shoulders in the way that drove him insane.

Kissing his way down her neck, he tried to explain. 'The guys have been alone on site for three days now. Who knows what sort of chaos they've got into?'

'How much worse could another half an hour make it?'

'Half an hour?' he asked. 'Is that all you want from me?'

She pulled back and gave him a promising grin. 'For starters. When you come back again… I might have other requirements.'

How was he supposed to resist that?

He let her strip the T-shirt from his torso altogether and shucked his shorts as he slid back between the covers with her again. The guys could wait another half an hour…

In the end it was more like an hour, not least because he had to shower again afterwards. Still, Liam reckoned he could get a couple of solid hours work in before the need to see Jenny again, to touch her again, became too overpowering.

'Okay, I'm really going this time.'

This time, she didn't try to stop him leaving.

Yawning, Jenny sat up, resting her back against the smoothed tree trunk that formed the headboard of the bed. 'Mmm… 'kay. Should I come too?'

He shook his head. 'Stay here. Eat some breakfast. Take a shower. Relax. I won't be long.'

'I should pack too,' she said, before yawning again. 'My flight's tomorrow.'

Something tugged inside his chest at the reminder, but he ignored it. The world was small these days. She might leave, but she could come back—or he'd go to her. They had an arrangement, after all. And, in less than six months, a child that would tie them together for the rest of their lives.

It was funny how that idea—which had been so terrifying to him a week ago—was almost a reassurance now.

He kissed her again and headed for the door, while she waved sleepily after him—lying down again before he'd even left the room, which made him smile. He'd worn her out.

He kind of liked that.

He'd expected to be plagued by thoughts of Jenny naked in bed, waiting for him, as he climbed down the twisting tree root stairs and headed for the main complex area. But, instead, different thoughts flew into his head, squawking like the macaws overhead, and every bit as insistent as the howler monkeys that still woke him every morning.

It was her comment about packing that had done it, he decided.

Of course she had to go. She had a job to get back to—as did he, since it was clear he wasn't going to give this project his full attention as long as she was here tempting him away.

It was just that the week had passed so quickly. He'd thought there would be more time to, well, talk. And admittedly spending the last two days in bed had cut into that time dramatically, but still.

They *had* talked, he supposed. About lots of things. Even beyond their past traumas and reasoning for avoiding love and happy ever afters.

In the darkness of their bedroom last night, for instance, they'd whispered all sorts of secret ideas of who they hoped their child would be—what elements of each of them he or she would take, physical and personality-wise.

'Mostly, I just want them to be themselves,' Jenny had murmured eventually, as sleep started to claim her.

'So do I,' he'd whispered back, as he'd kissed the crown of her head and watched her fall asleep.

So yes. They'd talked.

But it was only now he was faced with the idea of her leaving that he realised quite how much they *hadn't* talked about.

It had been so easy to just exist in the bubble of their bedroom, making the most of their time together. But at some point they were going to have to deal with the more complicated questions.

Like where they'd each live. How much

time they'd spend together. Whether the baby would move between their homes, or if he'd go stay with them whenever he was in LA. How parenthood would work around both their jobs. Would they need a nanny? He assumed so. How did that even work?

Suddenly, joking about ridiculous names, or whether the child would have his eyes, didn't seem quite so comprehensive as planning for the future went.

I hate planning for the future.

Because it never went the way he expected it to, anyway, so what was the point?

But a child…a family…that was going to take some planning. And Liam didn't have the faintest idea where to start.

There's time for all that.

Once Jenny had headed home to LA they could talk about it—by phone or email. It would be easier, he was sure, when they weren't able to get led astray by the temptation of their bodies.

Everything would be fine, he assured himself again as he spotted his site manager crossing the clearing towards him, clipboard in hand.

For now, he just needed to focus on his

work, and worry about his family later. Compartmentalisation was what had got him this far—putting his past behind him, saving the future for when it happened and focusing on the here and now.

And the here and now looked like it had its own problems to solve, from the frown on his site manager's face.

Jenny woke up again a while later, still alone, and lay for a long moment staring at the wooden branches of the treehouse ceiling. After two days, more or less, of constant Liam, the silence around her felt deafening. Her body felt abandoned without his fingers trailing over her skin. Even her voice, when she tried it in the empty room, was husky, as if there was no point in using it if he wasn't there to hear.

'Right,' she told herself, sternly and aloud. 'That's quite enough of that.'

She forced herself up and out of bed and headed for the shower, making mental lists as she went. She didn't have time to moon over a man—even one as spectacular in bed as Liam. She had work to do, and a future to fix.

Her job as Winter's PA had trained her to

plan the work, work the plan—and expect changes. As such, Jenny never made only one plan—she always had a backup at the ready.

When she'd arrived in Costa Rica, her plan had been to tell Liam about the baby, then head out if he wanted nothing to do with her and spend a few days holed up in a hotel in the city, taking long thinking walks and deciding exactly how she wanted her solo parenting future to look, and figuring out what she needed to do to make it happen, before she went back to LA and told her boss.

Obviously, that plan had changed. Plan B had been giving Liam the time he needed to figure out *his* next move and using the time to get to know each other. *That* plan, at least, had gone as it was supposed to.

But, distracted by Liam, she'd failed to figure out exactly what happened next. And with her flight leaving tomorrow, she needed to get onto that. Fast.

She couldn't go back to LA and tell Winter about the baby without at least the semblance of a plan. She needed to know, as a minimum, if she was going to be able to keep on working in the job she loved.

What if he expects me to move to Costa Rica? Or wherever his next project is?

She shook her head. Liam knew she wasn't the sort of woman to follow a man around the globe. He'd work with her on this.

But she still needed to figure out exactly what she wanted their co-parenting future to look like before they could discuss it.

Showered and dressed, she settled back into the chair on the balcony, Tarot cards, notebook and pen on the table in front of her. Crossing her legs under her, she closed her eyes for a moment and let the sounds of the rainforest soothe her tangled mind. The breeze in the leaves. The birds overhead. The insects chirping and buzzing around the flowers. Something larger moving through the branches of a nearby tree—maybe a monkey, or even a sloth.

She opened her eyes and smiled at the beauty and wonder of her surroundings, her heart already calmed.

Then she reached for the cards.

What do I want from my future? she asked them silently, holding the worn and battered cards in her hands. For a moment, she could almost feel that her grandma was there, watching over her shoulder as she shuffled them.

But when she drew her first card she couldn't make sense of what it tried to tell her. She squinted at the image of the Four of Wands. Usually that meant a celebration—even a wedding. Just what they'd each promised they weren't looking for.

Unless maybe he just didn't want to marry *her*. No. Jenny shook the thought away. Liam wasn't looking for commitment or marriage and neither was she.

But what if he met someone new and that changed?

She turned the card face down on the table and reminded herself that Tarot cards couldn't really tell the future. All they could do was give her clues to interpret her own state of mind.

And she did *not* want a big wedding and a happy family and everything that card represented.

She turned over the next card and sighed as the lovers stared back at her.

This wasn't helping.

Shoving the cards back into their bag, she opened her notebook instead and started to write—just a stream of consciousness of everything she was worrying about. What did she want from Liam, and their co-parenting arrangement? What sort of a mother did she want to be? What mattered to her most, and where was she willing to bend?

The words came easily now she was focused on what mattered, and she wrote until her hand ached. Pages and pages of thoughts and fears and ideas and hopes and dreams. Not about marriage or happy ever afters, but about a fulfilling, energising life and relationship with her child.

Finally, she put down her pen and smiled out into the darkening trees.

Wait. Darkening?

She'd grabbed a light lunch from the fridge earlier, but now it must be approaching dinnertime. And Liam still wasn't back.

Packing up her things, she stowed them back in the treehouse and headed out to see where he'd got to—and what he wanted to do about dinner. They'd talked about going out, but there was always the chance they'd just end up with takeaway in bed again...

She skipped down the stairs that spiralled around the tree and headed back towards what would, eventually, be the centre of Liam's latest retreat resort. It was easy enough to track him down; his site manager, who she'd been introduced to earlier in the week, was frowning at a clipboard as he pointed her absently in the direction of one of the treehouses currently under construction.

Jenny crossed to where he'd indicated and stared up at the large tree that formed the centre of the structure. She could wait until he came down, she supposed. Or else—

She spotted the ladder leading up to the next tree, and the temporary rope bridge leading across to the treehouse, providing access until the staircase was built.

Maybe she could just go and surprise him…

Liam had lost track of time, debating the latest issue in the current treehouse build—something that had taken a lot of explaining by the team who actually knew what they were doing because, while he was a very successful businessman, and had plenty of experience of working on traditional structures, building hotel rooms in trees had consistently thrown up far more problems than he'd ever imagined were possible.

Still, after a long afternoon's discussion, and some phone consultations with the experts, they finally had an answer to the issue that had been thwarting them all day. Which meant he could head back to *his* treehouse and take Jenny for dinner. Finally.

He clapped his lead builder on the back and took his leave, turning towards the opening that would eventually be a door. The stairs up to the treehouse were still to be built, but the temporary rope bridge they'd put up the day Jenny arrived led across to the linked platform they were using as a base while they were building.

But before he could take a first step onto it he realised there was already someone else crossing towards him.

'Jenny!' He smiled at first at the sight of her—and she looked up and beamed back. But the way she was gripping onto the rope that served as a handrail, and the paleness of her complexion, didn't look quite right. Frowning, he stepped forward, reaching out towards her as the bridge swayed under his weight. 'What's the matter? Is everything okay?'

'I'm fine,' she said, shaking her head to dismiss his concerns. Except, as she did so, the bridge swung a little more from side to side. And Jenny turned paler, her knuckles white as she held the rope on either side of her.

'Are you sure?' He moved closer, just as she took another step.

And then it felt as if the clock slowed— just enough to give him ample time to register every awful moment of each second that passed.

Jenny's foot slipped against the wooden plank of the bridge; damp from a brief shower of rain not long before, it had little grip under the soles of her sandals. Her foot, then her leg slid off the edge of the rough and ready bridge, through the gaps in the ropes that covered the sides, even as she gripped tight to the handrail.

And in that instant all Liam could see was history repeating itself.

He'd done it again. He'd brought a woman to danger and disaster, all because she'd followed him to this place. Because he hadn't been careful enough when they were in Iceland. Because he couldn't resist her. Because he hadn't just sent her away the moment she'd arrived—told her that he could only be bad for her, and for the baby, and they'd be better off without him.

Because he'd dared to think for a moment that he could have this—be a father, even with the caveats he'd put in place—Jenny was in danger.

It was such a long way down...

Her scream cut through the humid air of the rainforest and, without realising he'd even moved, Liam found he'd crossed the metres between them and hauled her up into his arms, huddling them both in the centre of the godforsaken rope bridge, desperately trying to keep her safe.

His heart hammered against his ribcage, his breathing harsh and uneven in the muffled silence of his blood pounding in his ears.

'I'm okay. Liam. Liam!' Jenny pulled at his hands and he loosened his grip a little but didn't let go. 'I'm okay, really. I just slipped!'

'You almost fell.' In his mind's eye, that was all he could see. Jenny, sliding out from under the inadequate ropes of the bridge, dropping the too long distance to the ground. Screaming for him to help.

If he hadn't reached her...

'But I didn't,' she said softly. 'The ropes

would have saved me. Liam. Let go. Come on, I want to get down from here.' She shuddered a little. 'I never did really like bridges. Especially ones that move.'

Neither did he any more. And he wanted her down from there more than anything. Moving was risky, but it had to be better than staying up there and taking the chance of her slipping again.

So, with a deep breath, he started moving, his jaw clenched tight. He kept a tight grip on her arm all the way back across the planks of the bridge, and down the finished staircase of the next tree, only releasing her when they both had their feet on solid ground again.

'Are you okay?' she asked, her forehead creased with concern.

'I should be asking you that.' His voice was shaking, he realised. As if *he* were the one who'd almost fallen.

Almost died.

Because she would have. No doubt. She said the ropes would have saved her, but what if they hadn't? What if one snapped? She'd have fallen. And from that height, onto the hard, tree root covered floor of the rainforest...

She'd have broken every bone in her body. And the baby...

They'd both have died. He'd have lost them both.

He'd have lost everything. Again.

God, he wanted a drink. Except that wouldn't help—it never had before. He was past that.

But he was also past putting himself in situations where his whole existence could be torn away from him in an instant.

Or he had been. Until Jenny came to Costa Rica and turned his life upside down.

'I'm fine,' she said now, taking his chin in her hand and forcing him to look at her. 'Look, I'm fine.'

'We should get you to the hospital. Have you checked out. The baby—'

'Is also fine,' she said, although how she could possibly know he had no idea. 'I didn't fall, Liam. You caught me. I barely even bruised myself. Come on. If you're done here, we can go back to the treehouse, decide where we want to go for dinner. Okay? I promise. Everything is fine.'

This time, he thought as he let her lead him back towards the treehouse he had claimed as his own. Everything was fine *this time*.

But what about next time?

CHAPTER THIRTEEN

LIAM WAS FREAKING OUT.

It wasn't as if she didn't understand a little bit. He'd been faced with the pregnant mother of his child being caught in an accident again—of course he was going to be a bit shaken. But this time, as she'd pointed out to him on the walk home, it was in no way his fault and, most importantly, she was absolutely fine. In fact, he'd saved her—although she maintained she'd have found her footing again even if he hadn't caught her up in his arms. She'd still had a good handle on the ropes, after all. And besides, the net of ropes that covered the side of the bridge would have caught her otherwise. Probably.

It was just a slip. She was fine.

Now she just had to convince him.

Which she intended to do over dinner, given the chance. She'd left him to shower and taken the opportunity to change into the dressiest item of clothing she'd brought with her—a halterneck jumpsuit that did marvellous things for her currently enhanced cleavage. If he planned on driving them down to that restaurant by the beach, she might even risk wearing her heeled sandals with it.

He was longer in the shower than usual, so she took her time over her hair and make-up too. When she took a last glance in the mirror, even she had to admit she cleaned up pretty nicely.

It was their last night together in Costa Rica, and she intended to make the most of it.

First, a nice dinner. Some flirtation and teasing to take his mind off that afternoon then, maybe, they'd be able to talk about some of the details of their co-parenting arrangement that she'd spent the day working out in her notebook.

Once they'd got all that straight, they could head back home to bed and *really* make the most of her last night. After all, she didn't know how long it would be before he could make it over to LA again.

Knowing that he would make it at some point helped, though. They would be a team.

And then there were all those benefits they'd been enjoying over the last couple of days…

Finally, everything seemed to be falling into place—against all the odds.

Before this week, she'd steeled herself against hoping too hard for anything. She'd prepared herself for going it alone because she knew that she couldn't trust anyone else to make the future she wanted for herself.

But now… Liam wasn't responsible for giving her the future she pictured; she still held tight control over that. But he was involved. A partner, even. And that made all the difference.

Jenny smiled at herself in the mirror just as Liam opened the bathroom door. She enjoyed the stunned look on his reflection for a moment, until she realised that he wasn't dressed for dinner. He was back in a T-shirt and shorts and, as the look on his face faded to confusion, apparently not planning to change.

'We talked about going out for dinner tonight?' she said, turning to face him.

'Yeah, right. We did.' He ran the towel over his head one last time, then tossed it behind him into the bathroom. 'I guess… I thought after this afternoon you'd want a quiet last night.'

She blinked at him. 'Liam, I told you. I'm fine. I didn't even get hurt.'

'But the shock…that can't be good for the baby, right?' He didn't meet her gaze.

There was something very wrong here.

'What's going on?' she asked bluntly. They'd never messed each other around before, and she didn't intend to start now.

Honesty and clarity. That was how they'd got this far. And now she needed some more of both.

He looked away. 'Nothing. I'm just…concerned for you.'

'That's not all.' Concern would be holding her, touching her, *looking* at her to check she was okay. This was something else entirely.

Oh, God, she realised suddenly. *He's changed his mind.*

She dropped to sit on the edge of the bed as the knowledge sank in. She didn't need him to meet her gaze. Didn't even need to hear the words—although she fully intended to make him say them, to make this real, to make him acknowledge what he was doing.

But the facts of it were clear even in the

silence. She could feel it, seeping into her bones, infecting her heart.

Just when she'd managed to trust enough to believe that they could do this, to put herself out there again to let someone else into her future, even if only as a friend and co-parent, he was about to turn the tables on her again. Just like Anthony had done when she'd thought they were going to get married. Just like her parents had when she'd let them down.

Her gut told her the truth, and she was a hell of a lot better at listening to it these days.

Liam wanted out.

The old her would have just watched him go. She'd have believed this was her fault, that she should have done things differently. And maybe she'd still have those thoughts later, once she was alone again.

But right now...right now she was going to make him explain to her exactly why he was doing this.

She needed honesty and clarity. One last time.

The self-loathing that had settled over him like an oil on the walk back to the treehouse hadn't washed off in the shower. Just the knowledge of what he was about to do made him feel unclean—and he knew that feeling wouldn't fade in a hurry.

Still, better to be a bastard now than let Jenny and the baby come to depend on him and *then* run.

Better to leave now and have them stay safe and sound away from him.

He couldn't be the man she needed. They needed.

He could only bring them pain, or danger, or both.

His actions had caused the death of the first woman he loved, and his unborn child. And maybe Jenny was right and she was fine after today's near miss, but that wasn't the point.

The point was, he lived a life incompatible with nice, safe, normal family life. With love and happy ever afters. With stability and ease.

She deserved that. So did their child.

What had he been thinking? Imagining that he could be what she needed?

Liam had pieced himself back together with parcel tape and string after the accident. Every day he followed the rules that kept him nominally healthy and sane.

He didn't drink. He didn't lose control. He didn't care too much.

He focused on what he could give to others from a distance—on building his business, on sending money home to the family farm from it, on giving people who needed it the safe space to regroup and recover.

He could send anonymous free breaks at his resorts to people he read about in the papers or on the internet who looked like they needed someone to give them a chance to put their lives back together. But he could never get close to those people or have them even know of his existence.

Because that way led to friendship, closeness, affection.

Even Josh and Winter, or his own family, he had to keep at arm's length, not letting them in too close, or too far. Because if he did…he'd lose them. He'd put them at risk—and himself, too. Because one more loss could be the thing that tipped him back over that edge he'd teetered on for so long.

He'd almost lost Jenny and the baby today on that bridge.

It had nearly stopped his heart, but it had also reminded him of the most unbreakable of all his rules, forged in the aftermath of the accident, when he'd just been trying to find a way to keep on living.

Don't care about anything so much that you couldn't survive losing it.

How had he ever deluded himself that Jenny and the baby would be any different?

Because you wanted her in your bed, not your heart, he reminded himself.

For all they'd promised to make their decisions without their libidos getting in the way, he hadn't, not really.

He hadn't been able to resist her, so he'd given her what he thought she wanted.

But he couldn't give her love. Or safety or security. Or a future that even remotely resembled the one she deserved.

Would she believe him, if he told her that? Would she understand, and accept it?

He hoped so. But he couldn't take that chance.

Which meant he had to lie.

'Liam.' Jenny looked up at him seriously from where she sat on the edge of his bed. The same place he'd left her lying naked that morning, waiting for him to come back.

He wished he'd known then that would be the last time he'd ever see her that way.

'Tell me what's going on,' she pressed.

He took a breath. 'I can't do this.'

She didn't crumple; that wasn't her way. Her back remained straight and strong, her face gave nothing away. Only the tiniest dimming of the light in her eyes gave any indication that she'd heard him at all.

'Can't do what, exactly? I need specifics.' The ice in her voice was unfamiliar; everything between them had always been so warm. Full of humour and affection and fun and attraction.

Not now.

'My site manager needed a meeting today; that's why I was gone so long.' Start with a truth, weave in the lie. 'There are some problems on the site here in Costa Rica, and the build is going to take longer than planned. Which means I'm going to need to spend more time here—and then I'll be straight off to my next project.'

'Next project?'

'There's a new site come up—perfect for my style of retreat resort. But I have to move quick if I don't want to miss the opportunity.' This bit was all lie. Oh, he'd had the odd meeting about possible sites, but he wasn't committing to anything yet. In fact, he'd planned not to, for a while. To get this place running, then spend some time with Jenny in LA, or wherever.

'Which means?' She knew. He could tell she already knew. But she was going to make him say it. Own it.

He couldn't blame her for that.

'I'm not going to have the time or the energy to be involved with the baby in the way we'd discussed.' Not that they really *had* discussed how it was all going to work. But his imagination had filled in the gaps in their conversations nicely, and he couldn't deny the slight wrench in his chest as he gave it all up. 'Really, I don't think it would be fair to you or them to be so unavailable and uninvolved, just swooping in when I had the chance then disappearing again.'

'So you're doing this for us, then,' Jenny said flatly.

He ignored her inference and ploughed on. He couldn't let her try to talk him out of this or point out the flaws in his arguments.

This wasn't about logic. This was about a

gut feeling. And every instinct he had was screaming at him to get out before he ended up in another situation that tore him apart and broke him for good this time.

'I think it's best if I'm, well, a silent partner of sorts,' he said. 'I'll support you financially, of course. But I don't want to be a part of the baby's life.'

'Or mine.'

God, it hurt to say it. 'No.'

What she hated the most, Jenny realised as she stared at him, was that she was *surprised* by this turnabout.

She shouldn't be. Everything she knew about men and relationships should have told her this was where it would end. Didn't it always?

He'd got what he wanted from her—had her back in his bed for forty-eight hours. And apparently that was enough. Why on earth would he want to saddle himself with her and a baby now?

Love always lets you down.

She knew that.

But she'd thought because this *wasn't* love, because they'd agreed it *couldn't* be love, that she'd be safe. That she could have this small sliver of happiness and support and not suffer for it.

How wrong could she be? Because having this rug pulled out from under her was already worse than realising how badly she'd been used last time around.

At least she didn't have to tell her family that she was going to be an unwed working single mother through choice, because they'd already disowned her for her last transgression.

And this one wasn't a transgression. It wasn't a mistake. It was her child and her life and her future and she would make the best possible life for the two of them that she could and damn everybody else.

Even Liam Delaney.

Especially Liam Delaney.

She just should have known better—that was the only reason she felt like crying. Because she'd wasted this week imagining a life that was never going to exist. Because she'd let herself believe in him, in them. Because she'd grown used to the idea of them being a team in this. That she wouldn't be alone.

She *wouldn't* be alone, though.

She'd have her baby. Her friends.

She'd be fine.

She just wished she'd remembered the brutal truths she'd learned about love and sex the last time around. Then she could have protected herself against this. That was all.

Liam was still talking—rambling on about transferring money to her accounts, about making sure her health insurance was good enough, about a house he owned somewhere in LA—but she wasn't interested in any of it. The details could wait—hell, they'd waited this long, hadn't they?

All she needed right now was to get out of here with her head held high and her dignity intact.

'That all sounds good,' she said calmly. 'But we can sort out the details when I'm back in LA and can talk to my lawyer. I'm assuming you'll want this agreement to be properly contracted and so on. Especially on the parental rights issue.' He'd agreed to sign them away if he wasn't involved, and she was going to hold him to that.

Liam blinked, looking slightly blindsided by her agreement. 'Right. Yeah, I guess we should.'

She nodded. 'Fine. I'll set up an appointment—we can do it by video call—and get it all sorted.'

'You're…okay with this?' His voice was cautious—as if he couldn't believe he was lucky enough to get away with this without a woman wailing and screaming at him. Begging him to stay. To love her.

Maybe that was what he was used to in his relationships—women who expected more than he was able to give and blamed him for his inability. But Jenny had known from the start that he couldn't do this, and yet she'd let herself hope anyway.

That was on her.

And there was no way in hell she was going to let him see that she was disappointed.

'Of course,' she said curtly. 'Honestly, I was pretty surprised when you said you wanted to try. I know this wasn't what you had planned for your future. Like I told you that first day, I was expecting to come here, tell you what was going on, then turn around again and leave to get on with it on my own.' She forced a smile. 'Looks like I was right about you all along.'

'I guess you were.' He returned her smile with his own uncertain one.

He didn't even realise she was lying. God, he was probably *relieved* she'd taken it so well.

And if Jenny got her way he'd never, ever know that she felt like she was dying inside right now.

CHAPTER FOURTEEN

HE FELT AS if he had whiplash. How had they got here? He knew it was his doing, but suddenly the situation seemed totally out of his hands as Jenny stood up and crossed the room to her suitcase.

'You know, I was thinking, now we've got the basics sorted, I might as well head back to the airport tonight, don't you think?' Her voice was calm and rational, everything he didn't feel right now. 'I can get a room at the hotel there and be ready for my flight tomorrow in plenty of time. I just need to pack up—do you think you could arrange a car for me? I've got the number of the airport transfer service who brought me here...'

He shook his head when she offered the card. 'I'll get one of my guys to take you.' That would be safer than an unknown driver on this difficult road.

And before he knew it he was outside, trailing down the staircase to find someone to drive her to the airport.

He didn't even consider taking her himself. She'd have suggested it if she wanted that. And besides, he didn't fully trust himself behind the wheel right now. His hands were still shaking.

He needed to centre himself. To do all those exercises he'd learned on his first retreat then avoided using unless strictly necessary. Most of the time he could keep himself under control through sheer willpower. But when things got bad he fell back on the tools that had saved him the first time.

The fact he needed to use them now was surely a sign that leaving Jenny to get on with her own life was the right decision. No one else had affected him this badly since the accident.

Of course, he hadn't let anyone else as close.

That had been his biggest mistake, he decided. If he hadn't let her in, it wouldn't hurt so much to push her away.

Better now than later, he reminded himself. *Better away but safe than hurt or dead.*

By the time he made it back to the treehouse with the news that the car was ready when she was, Jenny was waiting for him by the front door, her fingers gripping the handle of her small suitcase, her backpack slung over her shoulder. She'd changed out of the outfit she'd been wearing earlier, into more comfortable travelling clothes, and her hair was pulled back in a simple ponytail, her face scrubbed clean of the make-up she'd applied before.

Just looking at her made Liam regret again the loss of that last night dinner, or a final night with her in his arms. But if he'd let himself have that…would he still have been able to let her go tomorrow?

He wasn't sure.

This is for the best.

'The car is waiting by the entrance,' he said, his voice husky. 'My site manager's driving you. He needed to head back to the city tonight anyway. He's ready when you are.'

Jenny stepped forward, her case trundling behind her. 'I'm ready now.' She reached up and pressed a kiss to his cheek. 'Thank you for a lovely week. I'm glad we had those last couple of nights together before I had to go. But from here on, I think we can manage most things over email and the phone, don't you?'

Liam forced a smile. 'Of course.' She understood what he'd meant, by stepping away—or else this was what she wanted too. From the way she'd taken it, he was starting to believe that must be the case.

They'd had their fun, their second chance at a fling, and now they needed to get on with their real lives. What was wrong with that?

'And now I'll get out of your hair!' She laughed, but there was something in it that sounded just a little bit brittle. Forced even.

Or perhaps he was just projecting his own emotions onto her.

Because as much as this was his choice, as much as he knew this was the right decision—the only one he could have made, in the end—it still felt like his heart had cracked inside his chest.

The hotel was dark and the lobby empty except for a young girl on the reception desk when Jenny arrived. She'd booked a room on her phone in the car, so check-in was quick and easy. In no time she was up in her small, no-frills room, listening to planes still taking off and landing not far from her window.

She placed her suitcase on the floor, dropped her backpack beside it and sat on the edge of the bed. It was comfy, at least, but she knew she wouldn't sleep.

If she slept, she might dream of Liam. And she couldn't risk that.

She had plans to make. Everything she'd worked out sitting on the balcony of the tree-house earlier that day—and, *God*, how was it still the same day?—that was all out-of-date now. She'd been imagining her future with Liam in it, as a partner if nothing more.

Although, she had to admit, in her head, he'd been a lover too. A co-parent, friend *and* lover.

Wait.

With a groan, she fell backwards onto the mattress and threw her arm over her eyes.

Of course he'd pulled away—she could hardly blame him. Co-parenting friend he slept with? Yeah, that sounded an awful lot like what they'd both promised the other they weren't asking or looking for.

It sounded like a marriage. Like commitment.

Like trusting the other to always be around and not screw things up.

And they both knew that neither of them was up to that. He couldn't give it and she couldn't trust it.

She knew from bitter experience that other people's weaknesses always led to betrayal and disappointment. It was absolutely for the best that she was out of this situation now and could focus on building the future *she* wanted.

Forcing herself to concentrate on what came next rather than what she'd left behind in the rainforest, Jenny got to her feet and fished her notebook and pen out of her backpack. After a moment, she reached back in and pulled out her grandma's Tarot cards too.

Maybe that was why she hadn't been able to get a good reading from them earlier. Because she'd been refusing to see what was right in front of her—that she was angling to build a life exactly like the one she'd said she didn't want. No wonder the Four of Wands had been taunting her—what she and Liam had planned had been a marriage in all but name. One with a built-in expiry date to boot.

But now she was seeing more clearly, right?

She used the kettle in the room to make herself a cup of herbal tea, then settled into the chair by the tiny table in the window at the end of her bed. From there, the wide glass windows looked out over the airport, and she watched the lights of the arriving and departing planes rise and fall against the night sky for a long moment, centring her thoughts.

Then she opened her notebook and started to read.

It was all there in her own handwriting. Everything she'd hoped and dreamed for with Liam, and their child. The dream life she'd thought, so briefly, that she wanted.

She'd been here before, though. That life wasn't the one she'd been handed.

So she needed to make the most of the life she did have.

Turning to a fresh page, she started a new list.

Things to do next:
  1) Tell Winter about the baby.

That would be hard; her boss would be happy for her, she was sure, but there was history there too that would complicate Winter's emotions. And that was before they even started on the logistics of making her job work as a solo parent.

  2) Find a lawyer.

She'd never really needed one before, but if she and Liam were going to come to an arrangement over how this worked, she'd need one. She didn't want Liam's money, although heaven knew he had enough of it to spare by all accounts. She'd happily work to look after her own child and, one way or another, she had faith she'd make it work—after all, she was lucky enough to have a Hollywood A-lister as her employer, so she was already in a better position than many women.

But she did want *certainty*. If Liam said he didn't want to be part of the baby's life, fine. She could accept that. But she didn't want him changing his mind in five years' time and confusing the hell out of their kid without her permission.

A lawyer would help her figure out what ground rules they needed to set, and what was a fair contribution, if Liam felt he wanted to make one—even if she suspected he'd only be doing it to assuage his own parental guilt.

3)...

What next? There were a million things to do before the baby arrived, she was sure, but until she'd done the first two it was hard to get moving on the other stuff. So much depended on the decisions they made about her job and Liam's remote involvement.

So maybe she just started there. Got the basics in place before moving any further.

Fine.

She nodded to herself and checked the time. Middle of the night in Costa Rica, but fortunately Winter was staying in a completely different time zone right now, and middle of the night for Jenny was already halfway into tomorrow for her boss in London.

As she held her phone in her hand, she ran through exactly what she needed to say.

Winter, I need to tell you something important. While we were in Iceland I had a fling with Liam Delaney and now I'm pregnant. I've told him, and we've decided together that it's best if he's not involved in the baby's life, or mine, although he says he wants to contribute financially. When we're both back in LA, can we sit down and figure out how we can make this work with my job? I love working for you, and I don't want to leave, but I accept we might need to consider some changes to make it all work.

That sounded sensible and put-together, right? As if she and Liam had approached this as adults—not falling into bed before she'd even been able to tell him about the baby, spending the better part of a week getting to actually know each other before falling *back* into bed, then parting ways when they realised that neither of them was actually capable of a functional relationship.

Winter would have questions, though. She could already hear her boss's voice in her head.

Jenny, are you in love with Liam?

That, at least, was easy enough to answer, she thought as she dialled Winter's number.

Of course not. We had a lot of fun together, and I like and respect him as a person, but a relationship between us just isn't in the cards. Of course I'm not in love with him.

How could she be when she'd just said goodbye to him for the last time?

Yes, she felt abandoned, again. Lonely, again. As if she'd fallen into exactly the same trap that love and family had set for her last time. She'd had her future and her support ripped away from her, the exact same way she had when Anthony had gone back to his wife and her family had disowned her.

She *hurt,* that much she could admit.

But that was understandable, wasn't it? Under the circumstances.

That was all. It didn't mean anything more.

The phone started to ring.

Falling in love with Liam Delaney would be absurd. Ridiculous. Making *exactly* the same mistakes all over again. She was better than that. She'd learned from her past errors. She'd protected her heart this time, so even if it hurt it wouldn't break her.

Still ringing.

Just because they had amazing sex. And because she could talk to him, in a way she never really did to anyone else. And because he cared about her and wanted her to be happy and safe. And they had the same ideals for their child—to be happy and themselves above all else. And because they laughed at baby names together, and because she could picture their whole lives together and it made everything brighter and better just having him there.

'Jenny?' Winter answered the phone at last. 'Is everything okay? I thought you were on holiday. Isn't it the middle of the night for you?'

Just because the idea of living her life without him, raising their child without him, made her shiver with the loss.

'Jenny?' Winter asked, sounding concerned. 'What's happened?'

There were tears running down her face, Jenny realised as she answered. How long had she been crying?

'I fell in love with Liam Delaney,' she said through her sobs.

CHAPTER FIFTEEN

THE IMPORTANT THING, Liam knew, was to get back into his routine. He needed the familiar cadence of his days, the purpose of doing things that mattered to him, to get back on track after the disruption of Jenny's visit.

Ever since the accident, routine and purpose had been what kept him moving forward at a reasonable pace, living in the present rather than looking back, or panicking about what the future might hold. That was what he needed now. To be in the present.

So, in the present of the following morning, he got up at his usual early hour, even though he hadn't really slept. He did his usual exercise routine on the balcony, listening to the sounds of the rainforest around him and letting them centre him. He breakfasted on fruit and toast and drank his two cups of coffee while reading the news on his tablet, just like always.

Then he looked up, expecting Jenny to be there waiting to ask him about their plans for the day, and had to pretend his heart didn't sink a little when he remembered she wasn't there.

That she wouldn't ever be there again. Because he'd sent her away.

It's for the best, he reminded himself, and went to shower and get on with his usual daily routine.

On site days, it was easy enough to keep busy and push Jenny and the baby out of his head. The evenings were a little harder, but he'd found ways to distract himself. He had practice with this, after all. He knew how to compartmentalise.

And if his staff found him grumpy and more difficult to work with than usual they didn't say anything—although the looks of concern they shot his way tended to say more than their mouths did, anyway.

Josh had called a few times in the days since Jenny left Costa Rica, which he assumed meant she'd told Winter everything. He couldn't know for sure, since he hadn't picked up the phone, or listened to the voice-mail messages. The texts he'd received also went unread for now. He knew himself, knew how he handled trauma. He needed space between himself and the event, and *then* he'd deal with it, and other people.

Trauma. Strange that he was equating the amicable decision not to be in a relationship of any sort with Jenny with the sort of life-destroying trauma he'd been through in the past. It *wasn't* the same, of course it wasn't. But the echoes and reverberations of loss always seemed to call back to that moment. Reminders could be just as hurtful as smaller, fresh traumas. Or something. He couldn't remember what the counsellor who'd told him that had said, word for word, but he did know what worked for him.

And for now it was avoidance.

His site manager looked genuinely relieved when, after almost a week of such avoidance, he had to go up into the rainforest to visit a few potential suppliers. First up was the hot springs yoga sanctuary, where Selena greeted him with a warm smile—and a gently rounded belly.

'Liam! No Jenny with you today? I wanted

to compare bumps…' She threw her arms around him for a sideways hug, and he felt the hard pressure of her pregnant stomach against his side.

'She had to go back to LA.' He stepped away as quickly as he could without being insulting. 'Congratulations! You didn't have that last time I visited, did you?'

She laughed. 'Last time, I was wearing a loose shirt. Did you not notice? I just looked podgy. But it seems to have popped out this week, so now I'm showing it off!'

'Well, congratulations. To you and Gael.'

'You already said that.' Selena peered at him with concern. 'Is everything all right? When does Jenny get back from LA?'

'She's not coming back.' Better to face it head-on, get the truth out there so everyone else could move on as well as he had. 'We don't have that kind of a relationship any longer.'

'But her baby—'

'Will be her baby. Now, are you ready to talk about schedules?'

Selena nodded cautiously at his abrupt change of subject but, as he'd hoped, followed his lead. After an hour or so of discussion, they had a working plan for yoga classes at the new retreat—and Selena had suggestions for someone who could cover her classes when she had the baby.

'I think this will all work out fine.' Liam got to his feet and held out a hand for Selena to shake. But instead she gripped it in both of hers and pulled him close. On tiptoes, she whispered in his ear, 'You know it's okay for you to be happy, Liam. You just have to choose it.'

'I'll see you next month,' was all he said in reply.

Back in the four-by-four, he stared out of the windscreen with his hands on the steering wheel for a long few minutes before starting the engine and heading off to his next appointment, though.

Thankfully, he thought as he pulled in to the coffee roasting café, this was a place Jenny had never visited with him. There'd be no memories of her beaming at him in the sunshine here, and no well-meaning but nosy friends to ask questions about her. That would help.

He slammed the car door behind him, drawing rather more attention from the customers sitting outside the café than he'd intended, and headed inside to find Raúl, the boss.

'Liam! Come try this new blend.' Raúl beckoned him over towards the counter. Out back, through the window, Liam could see visitors roasting their own coffee beans to try. Jenny would have enjoyed that, if she hadn't been pregnant. If she'd come back after the baby—

He forced a stop to that train of thought. She wasn't coming back here. Not ever. And that was good.

The new coffee was delicious, and Liam enjoyed a catch-up with Raúl on how business was going. He liked to work with local businesses wherever he set up a retreat, and he was pleased to think that his resort would help Raúl and his family keep their business going.

'Papá!' A small boy came darting out from behind the counter, latching onto Raúl's legs where he sat on the high stool beside Liam.

'Santiago, this is my friend Liam,' Raúl said gently. 'Would you like to say hello?'

The boy peered out around his father's legs, took in Liam in a head-to-toe look, then shook his head.

Raúl laughed, and even Liam managed to crack a smile. 'Well, okay then. I think Mamá is looking for you anyway,' he added, glancing over Liam's shoulder.

Liam looked around and saw Raúl's wife, Maria, bustling towards them. Her dark hair fell in waves over her shoulders, her lush lips were curved in a smile and her eyes danced. But the thing Liam noticed most was the way her pregnant belly entered the room a good few seconds before the rest of her.

Is everybody pregnant suddenly?

Logically, he knew that Maria must have been pregnant the last time he'd seen her, probably a month or two ago, as she'd been away visiting family when he last came to the café. But it hadn't registered with him then, or he hadn't considered the information important enough to remember.

But now…now every child, baby or pregnant woman was a reminder of the life he'd sent away.

Maria led Santiago back into the rooms behind the bar, where he was supposed to be eating lunch, apparently. Raúl kissed his wife on the lips before she went, his hand lingering on her pregnant belly. Liam looked away.

'Only another few weeks and there'll be four of us, not three,' Raúl mused as they left. 'It's going to be chaos.'

Liam laughed, but only because he could tell from his friend's tone that he was looking forward to that chaos. Embracing it, even.

'Congratulations, if I haven't said it already.' Liam raised his coffee cup in a toast.

'Thank you. We're so excited!'

'I can tell.' Even if he couldn't understand. How could Raúl embrace such uncertainty? There were so many things that could go wrong every moment. Loving his wife and his children the way he did...what if he lost them?

Having had his own heart crushed by that loss, Liam knew the bravery it took to risk that. And while he admired his friend for being able to do it, he wasn't sure he'd ever understand how he could be *happy* about it.

'Don't you worry about them?' Liam blurted out the question without thinking first, and was surprised by the knowing look his friend gave him in return.

'Every moment,' Raúl admitted, his expression suddenly sober. 'Loving Maria, and Santiago, and the new little one...it's as if my heart resides outside of my body, with them. So yes, I worry.'

'But you risk it anyway,' Liam said. 'Why?'

'I love them.' Raúl shrugged. 'So how can I not? Besides, I know how much poorer my life would be without them.'

'You'd still have your business. Your work.'

'But what would it mean, without them? This is why we do it, isn't it?' Raúl said with a wide smile. 'The ones we love—family, friends, our people—are what give meaning to the work, don't you think? And everything else, of course!'

A tour group arrived at the door and Raúl slipped from his stool to go greet them, leaving Liam alone with his thoughts. Which was just as well, as it seemed, all of a sudden, he had far too many of them.

It was good to be back at work, Jenny told herself as she surveyed the hustle and bustle of the film set. Surrounded by people and action, kept busy and active, all of it distracted her from what had happened in Costa Rica.

Which didn't mean she was ignoring the future. Quite the opposite.

Winter had been brilliant. From the moment

Jenny confessed all, her boss had been her biggest cheerleader. She and Josh had hurried back to LA to meet her flight, and together the three of them had figured everything out.

In a matter of days Jenny had a lawyer who specialised in custody agreements, recommendations for three of the best day cares in the city, plus two excellent nannies to interview, and a request had gone out to headhunters to find her an assistant.

'You already do the work of about three people,' Winter had pointed out. 'If we get someone else in to take the admin stuff off your desk, you can focus on the things that no one else could do—like really managing my and Josh's careers.'

Jenny had blinked. 'That sounds like a promotion.'

Shrugging, Winter had grinned. 'I'd better give you a pay rise then, hadn't I?'

So now she had a plan, and Jenny was finally starting to relax again about the future. Unfortunately, when she wasn't kept busy by work, that just gave her more time to think about the things her plan *didn't* include.

Like grandparents. Or a father.

Not thinking about Liam.

That was a rule she'd imposed on herself—and she'd asked Winter and Josh not to talk about him either, at least for the first little while. Her hormones were crazy enough with the pregnancy, and she really didn't need anything else setting her off when she was trying to be professional.

She suspected that Josh had tried to contact Liam, though, after Winter told him what was going on. Josh could be kind of protective that way sometimes, she'd learned. But if he'd spoken to his friend he hadn't told her what Liam had to say.

What else *was* there to say, anyway? Jenny was pretty sure they'd covered it all in their businesslike farewell.

She was on her own raising their child, and she'd probably never see him again. Just get the occasional guilt cheque to cover expenses.

And she was fine with that. Really.

Apart from the thing where she was madly in love with him and her heart hurt every day thinking about how she'd given up and walked away.

But what was done was done, and she had too much pride to try and convince a guy to change for her. She'd done that last time, and look where she'd ended up. She wasn't getting on her knees to beg a man to stay ever, ever again.

Liam had been honest about what he could offer, and it had never included love. So what right did she have to ask for it?

With a sigh, she forced herself to focus on the activity going on around her. Josh and Winter were starring in their first movie together since their reconciliation, and it was kind of a big deal—not to mention a last-minute one. Josh had already been slated to star as the romantic hero of the piece when the actress originally cast opposite him had to drop out. Getting Winter in for the role had been a no-brainer for anyone who followed Hollywood gossip and had an inkling of an idea how big it would be for them to appear on screen together again.

But it did mean a lot of press interest, and requests for interviews and so on. While the movie of course had its own publicity team, and Winter hired professionals herself as needed, she liked Jenny to go through the requests personally and pick the ones she thought were the best fit for the brand Winter was trying to project.

Also, the ones with interviewers that wouldn't drive Winter crazy. Jenny had a sprawling spreadsheet of every journalist who'd ever spoken to Winter, every photographer who'd taken her photo, and notes on the results. She noticed there were one or two requests she could throw out immediately, according to the second sheet of 'publications and websites I will never work with again' she and Winter had put together based on their coverage of her and Josh's split five years ago.

She was just starting to get into a groove, coming up with a list of possibilities to go through with her boss later, when a hush on the other side of the set caught her attention. She looked up, frowning, as the initial silence shifted into a buzz of chatter and excitement.

What the hell was going on over there?

Placing her notes on the table in front of her, Jenny stood up to get a better view of what was causing the furore. And as she did she spotted a familiar dark head breaking through the crowd gathered behind the cameras.

Liam.

CHAPTER SIXTEEN

LIAM BRACED HIMSELF as he stepped through the doors onto a film set for the first time in five years, knowing the busyness and the noise and the lights and cameras were a full world away from the life he'd been living in the rainforest of late. Not to mention the memories that just being back on set would throw at him.

He sucked in a deep breath and reminded himself why he was there. His purpose today mattered more than his past anyway.

This was about his future.

Getting in had been easy enough—a quick call to a suspicious Josh, whose fears he'd allayed as best he could with a few assurances and a promise to explain everything *after* he'd spoken to Jenny—and he was in.

Dealing with the stares, the whispers and the attention was quite another thing.

He could feel everyone's eyes on him as he thrust his hands into his pockets and walked as nonchalantly as he could across the studio. He'd been an actor once. He could at least *act* as if none of this was bothering him even if, in truth, his heart was jackhammering so hard at what was to come he suspected they could use it as a sound effect.

Then he spotted Jenny, frowning towards the crowd, eyes probably narrowed behind her black-framed specs. Her hair was up in a familiar high ponytail, a few blonde strands framing her face, and she had a pen shoved behind her ear. There was no obvious outward sign of her pregnancy, but Liam noted—after Selena's comments—that she was wearing a looser, more flowing top than she usually favoured.

He paused for a moment and looked at her, letting the truth of what had brought him back to LA really sink in.

It was that pause that was his downfall, though, because before he could start moving again towards Jenny, someone grabbed his arm in a vicelike grip and began dragging him back towards the doors.

'Winter!' He tried to free his arm from

her biting fingernails, but without any luck. 'What are you doing?'

'Stopping you from making things worse.' She shoved him outside the doors to the studio set they were filming in. He could see the trailers the stars used between shoots off to the side, but he didn't imagine he was going to be invited in to Winter's for a cup of tea. 'Did Josh know you were coming here?'

'Um…' Liam winced and tried to decide whether dropping his friend in it would make things worse or better.

'He did, didn't he?' Winter's hands balled up into fists. 'Oh, I'm going to *kill* him!'

'Please don't,' Liam said. 'Jenny and I went to a lot of trouble to get you two back together in Iceland. Killing him would ruin that effort rather.'

'*You* got us together? You insufferably arrogant man.' Winter took a step closer, rage burning in her eyes. 'As if you know the first thing about love. If you did—' She broke off and Liam waited, curious to see if she'd finish the thought.

When she didn't, he murmured, 'Maybe I'm learning.'

Her eyes grew wide and she stopped short of

shoving him against the wall. 'Liam,' she said, her voice suddenly softer. 'Why are you here?'

'I'd rather talk to Jenny about that before you, if that's quite all right.'

'Then we'd better get this over with, hadn't we?' said a voice from behind him, and every muscle in his body tensed—especially his heart.

Jenny.

'Do you want me to stay?' Winter asked in a loud whisper as Jenny moved towards her.

Jenny shook her head. 'I can handle this.'

At least she hoped she could. Just seeing him again, breathing the same air, watching him move, was sending her mind and body into overdrive.

Hormones. Just blame the hormones.

Except it wasn't just the pregnancy hormones, she knew, because this had happened in Iceland too—long before she was willing to accept what it might mean.

When Liam Delaney was in the room she couldn't look anywhere else. Couldn't *think* about anyone else.

Which, of course, was exactly why he had to leave.

Fast.

Winter stepped away, but only as far as the studio entrance, keeping the curious crowd of onlookers at bay by shutting the large doors in their faces, which Jenny appreciated. They were probably holding up filming since their female lead was out here playing bouncer, but right now she didn't care.

She had some things she needed to say to Liam Delaney, and then he would leave again and she could go cry for an allotted ten minutes then get back to work.

That was her plan for the immediate future, and she intended to follow it to the letter.

'Liam, if you're here to change your mind, to renegotiate our agreement about the baby, you're wasting your time,' she said firmly. 'I won't be messed around like this. You showing up every time you feel guilty isn't going to help anybody—not me, not you, and certainly not the baby.'

'I know—' he started, but she cut him off. This was her time to talk.

'You wanted out of this situation, and I gave you that. No fuss, no demands—nothing. I gave you everything you wanted, and now it's your turn to give me something.' She drew a deep breath. 'Since you're in town anyway, I want you to meet with my lawyer and sign over all parental rights to me, like we agreed. That way I can be sure about what my future holds.'

'Nobody knows that for certain, Jenny.' His voice reverberated through her, as if her body was reacting to the memory of all the secret things he'd whispered to her over their nights together. She forced herself to ignore it. 'Trust me. I know. I spent the past five years trying to make my life as safe from change or disaster as possible. And then you showed up and blew that all away in less than a week.'

'Well, I'm very sorry if contraceptive failure has ruined your life, Liam, but—'

'That's not what I meant.' Why was he smiling? Shouldn't he be angry with her? Or guilty or sad or something—anything other than smiling gently at her.

She couldn't take his smile. Not today.

'Then say what you *do* mean and leave. Please.' She needed to get out of here. Away from him.

She needed to get back to work and focus on the future she was building for herself and her baby. A future without Liam Delaney in it.

He stepped closer and reached out to take her hand—but she yanked it back out of his reach. If he touched her… She needed to keep distance.

'I can't give you a perfect vision of the future, Jenny,' he said softly. 'But if you'll give me ten minutes, I'll give you all the certainty I have.'

There was something in his eyes. A seriousness blended with hope that made her nod without even thinking about it.

Oh, this could be a huge mistake. But somehow, Jenny couldn't stop herself from making it.

'You can use my trailer,' Winter called from the doors, giving up the pretence that she hadn't been listening in all along.

Jenny swallowed and attempted to mentally prepare herself. 'Come on, then.'

Liam knew this was his last chance—his only chance—to put this right. If she sent him away after this…well, he'd have to accept that. to sign over parental rights and let her build the future she wanted. Without him in it.

God, he hoped she didn't send him away.

Jenny shut the trailer door behind them and leant against it, even as she gestured for him to take a seat. Preserving her escape route, he assumed. In case she didn't like what he'd come here to say.

'So talk,' she said. 'Why are you really in LA?'

'Because I realised, after you were gone, it was already too late.'

'*What* was too late?' she asked, frustration colouring her voice. 'Liam, I don't understand.'

He gathered his thoughts as fast as he could, wishing he could remember all the clever things he'd decided to say on the plane. But they'd all rushed out of his head the moment he'd seen her again.

'I pushed you away because I was trying to protect my heart,' he said finally. 'After I lost Julie and the baby... I thought I'd lost everything. It took so damn long to piece myself back together again, and I thought the only way to keep me that way, to avoid ever being torn apart like that again, was to make sure I never fell in love again. To never care about anything or anyone that could be taken away from me.'

'I can understand that,' she said softly. 'I think I did something similar, for a long time.'

He looked up sharply, meeting her gaze, wondering if something had changed since they'd said goodbye. If their time apart had made her realise some of the same things he had. If maybe, just maybe, she was ready to give this—give him, them—a chance.

'But I realised it was too late,' he said. 'When you slipped on the bridge… I think I knew then, but I was too scared to face it. So *terrified* of losing you and the baby that I—'

'Sent me away.'

'Yes. Because I thought, somehow, that if I wasn't in your life you'd be safer. And that if you weren't in mine I could go back to living the same safe, emotionless life I'd been living for the last five years.'

Jenny pushed away from the door and took a step closer. 'So what changed?'

'I did,' he replied. 'When you were gone… that same life I'd lived before didn't feel safe any longer. It just felt empty. I missed you, and I missed the future we'd talked about and…' His eyes burned with unshed tears as Jenny moved closer again, perching on the small table in front of him and taking his hand in hers. 'I realised that living in this world, knowing that you and our child were out there, but not being part of your lives, not loving you, cherishing you, celebrating you the way you both deserved…that would be far worse than any other existence I could imagine.'

Jenny blinked at him. 'You love me?'

'With all my heart. You and our baby.'

She looked away, and he squeezed her hand to let her know he wasn't done yet. 'I can't tell you what the future will bring, and I can't make promises about it because I know too well that the future can change in the blink of an eye. But I can make promises about my heart, because that belongs to you and to our child.'

He swallowed and forced himself to say the scariest line he'd ever had to say which, given how many horror movies he'd starred in, was really something.

'So if you still want me, I am all in. Not just as co-parents, but as a family. Because I'm going to let myself love you both as much and as long as the world allows.'

His words were both barbs and salve for her battered heart.

Barbs because, just when she'd thought she

had her future planned out, he'd thrown it all into disarray again. He'd brought uncertainty back into her life just when she'd been certain, and when she needed that certainty more than anything. Or so she'd thought.

Because that salve...he loved her. And she loved him too. Loved him so much her heart ached with it, and hearing he felt the same soothed that pain.

He was right; he couldn't make promises about the future. Nobody could. And just like him she'd worked so hard to stop history repeating itself that she'd run away from him at the first sign that things wouldn't work out. She'd put up all those walls she'd only just begun to let down after finding her place in LA.

After finding him in Iceland.

Being with Liam in Iceland, even in a purely physical relationship, had started her on the path to opening herself up again, she realised now. To realising that she could have pleasure, and fun—even happiness, on her own terms.

Spending time with him in Costa Rica, though...that was when she'd seen the whole of him, his heart and soul for the first time.

That was when she'd fallen in love.

'You're right,' she said, her voice husky in the stillness of the trailer. 'You can't promise me anything about the future. No one can—not even Grandma's Tarot cards. The future will always be uncertain. It will always be a risk.'

'Jenny—' he started, but she shook her head to stop him. She wasn't done yet.

'But what being back here in LA without you has taught me is…you are worth taking the chance. The life we could build together with our child, however that ends up looking, that's not a risk. It's *everything*. Everything that matters to me. And I want to see where we end up.'

Maybe she could stand a few surprises if she had Liam at her side. If she knew what she was battling through the uncertainties for—her love, and her family.

'Do you mean…' He trailed off, as if afraid to say what he was hoping for.

Standing up, Jenny tugged on his hand until he was standing facing her, then smiled at him.

'I mean… I know you're scared of the future. So am I. And we've both been given good reasons to be cautious about love and everything that it brings. But…maybe it's time we were scared *together*. What do you think?'

Liam returned her smile with a warm grin of his own. 'I think that if we can face the future hand in hand, we can face anything. Together.'

As he kissed her, Jenny heard a muffled whoop of joy from outside the trailer and realised that Winter had probably been listening in the whole time. Hell, she was probably planning the wedding already.

But then Liam deepened the kiss, and she forgot to think about anybody, or anything, outside the wonderful future she was going to build with the man she loved by her side.

EPILOGUE

THERE WAS A howler monkey somewhere near, calling from the trees. Liam smiled at the sound of it, even as his best man startled and looked around, trying to find the culprit.

'What was that?' Josh asked, looking alarmed.

'Howler monkey,' Liam said. 'Nothing to worry about.'

'Right.' Josh continued to nervously watch his surroundings. Liam supposed that, for a farm boy from middle America, used to wide open plains and crops, the dense foliage and amazing animals of the Costa Rican rainforest must be a bit of a change of pace.

The treehouses that formed the backbone of his retreat resort were all built now, solid wooden staircases that wound around the trunks leading to luxury spaces in the canopy where a person could think, reflect and reconnect with the natural world.

Today, the balconies were hung with bunting and ribbons and the clearing at the centre filled not with tourists but with his and Jenny's friends, and even his family.

But no Jenny. Not yet.

'Did you ever imagine you'd end up here?'

'In the rainforest? No.' Liam craned his neck, searching for his bride.

'I didn't mean…well, I suppose I did, a bit,' Josh said. 'Costa Rica is pretty incredible. But no, what I *meant* was…when I got my second chance with Winter, it was more than I ever believed I deserved or was even possible. And for you…you were always so adamant that you didn't want this—marriage, a family, all of that. Did you ever really imagine you'd end up here?'

And then, from between the trees, Winter appeared in a bright red sundress, and the crowd began to settle. From somewhere, music started to play and Liam felt his heart speed up as he watched the gap in the trees until…

Jenny. She stepped out, her white halterneck dress glowing in the sunlight as it hugged her curves before flaring out into a skirt that ended halfway down her calves. Her blonde hair was pinned up off her neck, her lips painted a rosy red, and she beamed at him as she made her way down the gap their guests had left for an aisle, Winter following behind.

Instead of a bouquet, she held their daughter on her hip, her head raised and her gaze inquisitive as it always was. Liam watched them draw closer, his heart full to bursting, before he remembered that his best man had asked him a question.

One that deserved an answer.

'I never thought for a moment I could be so lucky,' he said as Jenny passed the baby to Winter and took the last couple of steps alone to join him in front of the celebrant. 'But then, the future always does have a way of surprising us, doesn't it?'

* * * * *

If you enjoyed this story, check out these other great reads from Sophie Pembroke

Vegas Wedding to Forever
Their Second Chance Miracle
Baby on the Rebel Heir's Doorstep
Their Icelandic Marriage Reunion

All available now!